Heartbeat Interrupted

A Novel By

Donelle Knudsen

Book Two
of the Heartbeat Series

I owe my love of books and the craft of writing to my late
father, Donald A. Williams, who encouraged and
supported me from day one.
I think about you every day, Dad.

CHAPTER 1
Touch Down

THE TIRES HITTING the runway set off Diana Baker's phobia. She twisted around in search of the nearest emergency exit. Her elderly seatmate smiled and patted her hand. "It's okay, dear, no matter how often I fly, I get heart palpitations when we land."

"Thank you, Mrs. Tripp, I'll be fine." Diana grasped the armrests and peered out the window as the plane taxied to the gate. The flight from Naperville, Illinois to Portland International Airport had been uneventful; however, her visit would be extraordinary. Diana was at the front of the plane and able to exit without a hitch. As she rolled her suitcase up the exit ramp, she felt lightheaded, tears filled her eyes, and her heart felt full to bursting.

This is it. I'm finally going to meet my family for the first time since my birth. She entered the terminal and scanned the crowd. Everyone looked the same, no one stood out ... until she saw a couple standing apart from the rest. Her mother was blonde and her father had sandy-red hair. They waved and ran toward her. It was clear they recognized Diana in a heartbeat.

Diana dropped her backpack on the terminal floor and fell into Emily's outstretched arms. James, her husband, edged in, encircled the women with his arms, and said, "No one will ever hurt us again. No one."

The airport crowd thinned, leaving the family huddled in the middle of the concourse. When Diana lifted her head, she saw the blue eyes that had visited her childhood dreams: her mother's eyes, which were now damp with tears of joy.

"I've waited eighteen years to hear your voice and see your beautiful face." Emily swallowed. "I almost gave up, but God told me to hold on even when all hope was gone."

"Mother." Diana leaned into the cleft of Emily's shoulder to fit like a puzzle piece and complete the perfect picture of mother and daughter.

James sniffled and pulled a crisp white handkerchief from his back pocket. He wiped his eyes and nose, looked around, and then said, "Maybe we should go, dear."

"Wait." Diana looked to her father. "I need a hug, too." She wrapped her arms around his waist. James rested his chin on top of his daughter's head before he pressed his lips against her soft cloud of blonde hair and breathed in. He stepped back to get a clear view of his long-lost daughter.

Diana covered her mouth and hiccupped; followed by Emily. Diana laughed at her private joke. *We're alike.*

The three strolled the concourse with arms entwined. The burgeoning crowd of harried travelers wove around them; some brushed their shoulders, a few frowned as they hurried on their way.

* * *

Once inside the car, Diana laid her head back on the headrest, closed her eyes, and sighed. *I'm finally going home like Dorothy Gale returning from Oz.* In the front seat, her parents' voices blended with classical music and lulled her into a deep sleep.

"Diana, we're almost home. Your brother and sisters can't wait to meet you," Emily said.

"What? Sorry, I kind of fell asleep."

Emily smiled. "Understandable. It was a long flight. You must be exhausted."

"I am, actually." Diana rubbed her eyes and tried to focus.

"After you get settled, we want to take the whole family to an early dinner and celebrate your homecoming. What is your favorite food?" James asked.

Without missing a beat, Diana said, "Hamburgers, french fries, and Coke."

"A girl after my own heart." James glanced at this wife. "Yes, siree, she's a girl after my own ..." He didn't finish.

"Concentrate on driving, dear." Emily patted his knee.

James pulled into the driveway. Diana leaned forward and peered between her parents to see twin girls, not much younger than herself, and a boy who looked ten or eleven.

The girls jumped off the porch, ran to the car, and left their brother leaning against the porch pillar with hands stuffed in his jeans' pockets. A frown wrinkled his freckled face.

Emily stepped out of the car and hugged the twins; she kissed their cheeks and brushed a tear from her eye. The girl in green shorts pulled away and pointed to the car. "Is this Diana?"

"Who else would it be, silly?" The twin in the yellow shorts jabbed her twin sister in the ribs.

Diana opened the door, swung her feet out, and paused before she looked up and met two sets of blue-green eyes. Kerri and Kate broke into smiles; each one held a lock of blonde hair in their forefinger and twirled it into a knot. *They do the same thing I do when I'm nervous.* Diana let out a giggle which broke the tension.

"I can't believe it," Kate said. "It's really you." She pulled Diana out of the car and into an embrace. Diana wrapped her arms around Kate and buried her face into her neck.

Kerri stood apart from the rest with her hand over her mouth and then, apparently feeling left out, joined her sisters to form a group hug.

James and Emily smiled as they watched, but Bryan hadn't changed his expression or left his post by the front door. He removed his hands from his pockets and crossed them over his chest.

* * *

After dinner, Diana sprawled on one of the twin beds in the upstairs guest room. Despite her sisters' urgings to sleep in their room, she begged off with a headache. The day had been a miraculous answer to prayer, but an intense emotional experience. The only cloud over the family's celebration had been Bryan's reaction to her homecoming.

She pictured his scowling face and the hostile looks he gave her between bites of his hamburger and sips of root beer. Now she was free to chuckle over him belching in the restaurant. That night, at home after dessert, Diana rose to take her plate to the kitchen, but waited at the door when she overheard him saying to his sister, "Who does she think she is, some kind of rock star?" All day long he had acted rude. She guessed he was jealous and resented her sudden appearance.

Diana rolled over and grabbed her cell phone from the bedside table. She stared at it and thought, *Even though it's pretty late there, I should call Kevin. Dad for sure. But I'm exhausted and there's so much to tell. I don't know where to start.*

When her phone rang, she dropped it like a hot coal. She saw her boyfriend's ID and grabbed it off the floor. "Kevin, I was getting ready to call."

"I couldn't wait any longer, babe. How are you? How was the reunion?"

Diana forced a laugh. "The reunion was pretty good, but now I'm about to lose it."

"Why?"

She flopped back on the bed and let out a sigh. "Let's say not *everyone* is happy to see me." Diana twirled a strand of hair into a knot.

"Who's the idiot?" Kevin sounded angry.

"Bryan. He's only ten and doesn't seem wild about sharing his family with me."

"Oh, he's only a kid. He'll get used to the idea." Kevin chuckled.

"I hope. Anyway, how about you, your job, college? Anything exciting going on?"

"No, you own all the drama. Can't wait until we're together again." Diana heard a kissing noise from the other end.

"Love you, too. I miss you." Diana stifled a sob.

"Me too. But this is *your* time and you need to spend it with your real family."

Diana sat up and felt a surge of anger. "Don't say *real* family like they're better than Dad. I'm excited to have them in my life, but we don't really know each other, yet."

"I'm sorry, Di. I didn't mean to hurt your feelings. It'll happen. And I hope it's real soon."

"Me, too." Diana rocked back and forth against the headboard. "I want to feel like I belong. And I miss Socks." She hiccupped.

"I wish you had me to cuddle instead of your kitty." Kevin laughed. "But you'll have them wrapped around your finger before long. Like me."

"You know the perfect things to say. I love you."

"Love you more. I'll let you get some sleep. Call as soon as you can," Kevin said.

After hanging up, Diana couldn't decide whom she missed more, Kevin or Glenn, the man who loved her and raised her as his own daughter for eighteen years. She desperately needed to hug someone, something. She rolled over on her side and grabbed the extra pillow.

Thoughts of Roberta, the woman who had posed as her mother for her entire life, surfaced like a boil on her neck. Sleep was long in coming and when she awoke at 2 a.m., she shivered from the dream of Roberta pushing her way back into her life. She remained stick-still, staring at the ceiling and wondering if her birth parents, James and Emily, would take Roberta to court or forgive the unimaginable sin of kidnapping their daughter from the hospital nursery so many years ago. She drifted off to sleep hugging the pillow and wondering what would happen in the next few days and weeks.

CHAPTER 2
Backup Plan

ROBERTA HAD MET IRMA in Pendleton, Oregon at the Rainbow Café during the drive home from the Oregon Coast. One conversation was all she needed to determine Irma was the perfect mark.

Roberta called Irma a few weeks later, gave a sob story, packed her belongings in her beat up Honda, and left her hometown of Boise. When she arrived on Irma's doorstep, she hoped she would take her in until she was able to get on her feet.

As Roberta waited for Irma to answer the doorbell, she wondered, *Will I ever see Diana again? I gave her the best years of her life, and this is the thanks I get. I hear she took off to Portland without as much as a goodbye. How could she desert me in my hour of need?*

Irma opened the door and appeared surprised to see Roberta, but her face lit up in a smile. "My, my, I didn't expect to see you so soon." Her hand fluttered at her throat. "I'm sorry, but I've forgotten your name."

Roberta couldn't remember the phony name she had given Irma over the phone two days prior, so she stuck to the truth. "Roberta."

"Of course, please come in." Irma widened the door and Roberta entered a new stage of her turbulent life.

* * *

Roberta heard Irma call from the kitchen, "Are you almost ready? You don't want to be late for your job interview today."

"Yeah, yeah," Roberta muttered as she pulled on navy blue slacks, looked in the full-length mirror, turned sideways, and sucked in her stomach.

"The coffee's made and oatmeal is on the stove. I have to leave for my shift at the Mill. Have a good day and best of luck," Irma said as she left.

Roberta squinted in the bathroom mirror and frowned at the wrinkles around her eyes. She applied makeup, braided her long black hair, and patted the extra skin under her chin. "If only I had the money for a facelift, I'd have no trouble getting a job. Or a serious boyfriend."

Wrinkles aside, she wasn't worried about her interview at a local café. She had no restaurant experience, but with Irma's recommendation and her natural gift of gab tucked away for good measure, Roberta felt self-assured. *It's a slam-dunk.*

* * *

That evening Irma and Roberta shared dinner in Irma's kitchen. "So how did it go?" Irma asked.

Roberta leaned back and tapped the ashes of her half-smoked cigarette onto her empty plate. "Good, I think it's in the bag. I'll hear for sure tomorrow."

"Sadie, the one you spoke with, is a friend and I'm sure she'll hire you no problem. With your looks and personality, I wouldn't worry, Roberta." Irma cleared away her dishes and then started the coffee machine.

"I hope so." She took another drag on her cigarette and held her breath for a few seconds before she exhaled.

"I'm glad I can help out, for a while." Irma coughed and cleared her throat.

Roberta glanced at Irma and wondered what conditions she had set on her living arrangement. In Boise, her friend, Zoë, had said she could stay on indefinitely. She chewed her lower lip in thought. *I've got to lay low for a while. Diana's lawyer, what was his name, John Bowen? He won't find me here. But who knows what her new-found family might do?*

"I believe blessings come to those who earn it." Irma held up a plate of home-baked cookies. "Like some with our coffee?"

"Sure, as long as I can fit into my jeans tomorrow." She ground out her cigarette on her plate.

Roberta believed in fate and had relied on Zoë's expertise as her spiritual advisor. "That reminds me. Are there any psychics, you know, palm readers in Pendleton?"

Irma sat down and tapped the side of her head with her forefinger. "Not sure. I'm not into that kind of thing. Let me ask around."

Roberta bit into a soft chocolate chip cookie. "Good." She wiped her lips, smearing chocolate on the cloth napkin. "Sweets. My only vice."

CHAPTER 3
Moving Forward

THE NEXT MORNING, Diana called Cassie, her best friend, who lived in Boise. She tried to keep the conversation lighthearted. "Hey, girl, how's cooking school going this semester?"

"Big news. I'm ramping up my training and applying to Le Cordon Bleu in Portland. Maybe we can hang out and do the girl-bonding thing. That is if you're still in Portland."

Diana sat up and pounded the mattress. "That's great! I will, I mean, I'll be here for a while. But can you leave? How's your mother feeling?"

Diana heard Cassie expel a long breath. "Mom's great, the cancer's officially in remission. And with her and Glenn talking every day, making plans, she's on cloud nine." Cassie chuckled. "I think they've moved to the next level. We're one step closer to being sisters."

Diana leaned back on her pillow. "Well, what do you know? Dad's been keeping secrets."

"I'm prejudiced, but *I* think they fit better together than him and his old girlfriend. What was her name?"

"Beth." Diana wrinkled her nose. "No kidding. I wish I could talk all day, but the family has plans to go to their beach house this weekend."

"Give me another sec. How is it going?" Cassie sounded concerned.

"Good. The twins, Kate and Kerri, are super and we look a lot alike. Emily and James, I mean Mom and Dad, are great. Bryan, the ten-year-old, isn't cool with the idea of *me*, yet."

"That's too bad, but he's been the baby of the family. Do you think he's jealous?" Cassie asked.

"Could be. Sorry, I gotta go. Give Maggie a hug. Love you, Cass."

* * *

Diana stood in the doorway of the kitchen and watched her mother wash the last of the breakfast dishes. It couldn't have been more different from her memories of Roberta standing in their kitchen, pouring pancake batter, cursing over how they looked, and throwing the spatula across the room into the sink. She didn't miss the smell of cigarette smoke, either.

Diana thought back to her seventeenth birthday. Roberta was in a vile mood. She spat out the words like venom: "The man you call Dad isn't who you think he is. He isn't your father. He didn't even adopt you. Glenn is only your stepdad."

After the shock wore off, Diana asked Glenn, who was a lawyer, to help find her birth father. It had been only fifteen months since that day, but to Diana it seemed like eons.

Diana broke her reverie and asked, "Mom, what can I do to help get ready for our trip?"

Emily smiled. "How about bringing in the picnic ware from the garage? You'll find the wicker basket, plastic plates, and such in the cupboard right outside the door." She paused. "Oh, and ask Bryan where the volleyball, nets, and the badminton set are kept. We always have friendly contests if the beach weather is good enough."

Diana wasn't looking forward to speaking with her brother. It had been a week, but he still made her feel uncomfortable. In the downstairs hallway, she nearly bumped into Bryan coming in from the backyard. He stopped short and gave her his trademark scowl.

"Sorry, I was in a hurry," Diana said.

He leaned against the wall and crossed his arms over his chest. "So, how long you gonna stay?"

"I'm not sure … it's only been a few days. I want to get to know everyone better and see the sights. We're going to the beach tomorrow." Diana smiled and twisted her ponytail into a curl.

"Well, duh. You think I'm dumb or something?"

Diana ignored his rudeness. "Mom, uh, Emily, wants to know where the volleyball and badminton things are."

"In the storage shed."

"Could you put them out for Dad to pack?" Diana felt hiccups coming on and swallowed hard, but her throat convulsed in protest.

Bryan laughed. "Mom hiccups when she's upset or mad. That's funny."

CHAPTER 4
Run Free

"KERRI, WE GIVE UP, you're the best," Diana cupped her hands around her mouth and shouted into the wind. She, Kate, and Kerri had started a friendly competition to see who was the fastest in the 100-yard dash. Twice a day they raced along the wet sand. Kerri won every time.

"Give it up, sis. I've only beat her a few times and I've been at it longer." Kate put her hands on her knees and leaned over to catch her breath. She stood and stretched. "Glad I have company in the loser's circle."

"I thought I was a pretty good athlete, but she's tough to beat." Diana laughed at the sight of Kate's long, damp hair blowing in the stiff coastal breeze. "Boy, you look a mess. Do I look as bad as you?"

"Thanks a lot. And, yes, you do." Kate giggled. "Who cares? Kerri will be back soon. She likes to run to the rocks. Hold on, I've got to get the sand out of my shoes." Kate slapped one shoe against her hand and shook it out. "May I ask you a personal question?"

"Sure." Diana swallowed a hiccup.

"What did you think of us? Were we like you expected?" Kate looked toward the incoming tide.

Diana followed Kate's gaze. "The lawyer sent me photos, but I guess you don't mean photos."

"No."

"On the flight out, I looked at the album and keepsakes your … our parents sent and I couldn't help but cry most of the way." She cleared her throat. "I had a feeling you and Kerri'd be sweet; Mom would be emotional; and Daddy would be like Dad, uh Glenn, strong but soft and mushy on the inside."

"And Bryan?" Kate asked.

"Bryan … well, when I saw him standing on the front porch the first day, I got the feeling he was *not* happy. And he's been giving me the cold shoulder ever since." She rubbed her left eye that started to twitch.

Kate nodded. "His behavior's embarrassing. Mom's talked to him and Dad told him to 'straighten up.' I think he'll come around."

"He isn't frowning at me as much." Diana laughed and stifled another hiccup.

"I'm glad." Kate smiled.

"Hey, guys, ready to race me back to the house?" Kerri returned and skidded to a stop. She put her hands on her waist and wiggled. "Ready, set …"

"Yup," Diana said. "But this time you're going to lose." She took off and left the twins convulsing in laughter.

* * *

Roberta's first week at the Rainbow Café didn't work out well. The tips were not what she had expected and she resented the locals who sat for hours drinking coffee and laughing at each other's corny jokes. Her boss rode her tail every minute.

"I know this is all new to you, Roberta, but we're like family at the Rainbow. You can't tell people to hurry up or ignore them when they want refills. That isn't us," Sadie said.

Roberta listened with one ear and watched Sadie wipe the counter as she repeated the Rainbow mantra. "Right, right. Can I go out back for a smoke?"

Sadie glanced at the clock. "Wait till it slows down. Around 2:30."

Roberta looked around and saw three booths with the same people from lunchtime and one couple sitting at the counter drinking beers. She thought it was odd to see beer served in the café, but Sadie had explained that besides the bar in the rear, alcohol could be consumed legally at the counter away from the booths.

"I have to make a phone call. Be right back." Sadie opened her mouth, but Roberta was already headed to the backdoor.

In the parking lot, Roberta called Zoë, her best and only friend. "Hey, how's it going in Boise?"

"Good, my friend, very good. How are you? Where are you living?"

"Pendleton, the hell-hole of Eastern Oregon. I got a job last week, but it sucks."

"I'm sorry. Maybe you can find another."

Roberta snorted. "Yeah, right. Have I gotten any mail, calls?"

"No, nothing. Have you heard from Diana? I'm worried about you two."

"We haven't spoken in a while." Roberta saw Sadie standing at the backdoor waving at her to come in. "Shit, the warden's on my case again. Talk to you later."

CHAPTER 5
Past Meets Present

DIANA ENJOYED every minute with her family at the beach house, but as soon as she returned to Portland, she called Glenn, the father-of-her-heart, who lived in Naperville. "So, Dad, how are you doing?"

"Not so good. The house is too quiet. Socks is moping around like she lost her best friend, which she has. We've been watching a lot of TV together the last two weeks. But she prefers your company to a middle-age guy who knows nothing about cats."

"I'm sorry. I wish Socks could be here, but it wouldn't work. I'm surprised you have time to sit around and watch television."

"How so?"

"I heard you and Maggie have been burning up the phone lines."

"And you heard this where?"

"Cassie spilled the beans."

"How do you feel about it, kiddo?"

"I think it's great, fantastic! Don't make any hasty decisions about giving her a ring, though."

"Good one. Sounds like advice I gave you and a certain young man a while back." Diana heard him clear his throat. "How are things going with your family?"

"Fine. We just got back from a long weekend at the beach house. The twins, Kate and Kerri, are totally awesome. We hung out the whole time and had really good talks, stayed up late, played cards. Emily and James are loving, but not smothery; and Bryan, the ten-year-old, is getting over his sulk, sort of."

"I'm glad. Have Emily or James said anything about how they want to handle Roberta?"

Diana fell back on the bed and stifled a hiccup. "There hasn't been time for any kind of serious talk. We just got back from the beach." She rubbed her twitchy eye. "The thought of Roberta gives me a headache."

"I can imagine."

Diana pounded her fist on the bed. "I'm done with her. *So* done."

"I'll update John. No need to start legal moves on our end, yet. But when and if the D.A. gets wind, it will be out of our hands. On a different note, how's Kevin?"

"Oh, Dad, you're getting personal." Diana laughed. "He misses me and I miss him, if that's what you want to know."

"You know dads. We have to run through the parental check list. Boyfriend, check. Now, about college. It's getting pretty late to register for fall term here."

"I know. I want to enroll, but so much is going on and I'm starting to feel like part of the family. Maybe winter quarter, after the holidays." Diana took a deep breath and held it as she waited for a reaction.

"I see. I don't mean to be pushy. Only testing the waters."

She slowly expelled her breath. "I miss you like crazy, Dad, but I hope you understand."

"I do. You need your space and time to think. Take care, Princess."

"Thanks, Dad. Say *Hi* to Maggie for me and I'll call in a couple days. Love you."

CHAPTER 6
Roberta

"ROBERTA, I HATE TO COMPLAIN, but could you help out a bit around the house?" Irma asked.

Roberta was sitting at the kitchen table, browsing through the classified ads, and smoking her third cigarette since breakfast. "In what way?"

"Well, helping with the laundry, putting dirty dishes in the dishwasher, wiping out the bathroom sink after you're done."

"Oh, I see. The honeymoon's over." Roberta dumped her cigarette in her coffee cup and leaned back.

"I like having you here, and all, but my house isn't very large and if we both keep things tidy, it's easier to manage." Irma gave a weak smile.

"I'll try." Roberta pointed to the paper. "I've been looking through the want ads. The Mill is hiring part-time in the Outlet Store. Know anyone who works there?"

"Yes, why?"

"I'm thinking of quitting the Rainbow. Tips are crap, the locals drive me nuts drinking coffee and sitting on their butts for hours; and Sadie is, well, I won't say what I think. She being your friend."

"Well, you can answer the ad, but this time I can't give you a leg-up."

"Huh." Roberta got up, took the paper, and left her breakfast dishes on the table.

She returned to her room, grabbed a cigarette and her silver lighter from the bedside table, and flopped on the bed. She flicked the lid with her thumb and lit the cigarette. Taking a drag on the cigarette, she inhaled deeply and breathed out slowly. Staring at the ceiling, she thought about her situation and cussed out loud about ending up in a tiny guest room in Oregon, alone and almost broke. "Damn, why do these things happen to me?"

Roberta's lips twisted into a smile as she thought about how she had duped Glenn into marriage. Unaware she had kidnapped baby Diana from a hospital nursery in Portland a few months before, Glenn had given them a stable home life and treated Diana as his own daughter. Their marriage ended eight years later; when Roberta received the divorce decree, she breathed a sigh of relief knowing her dark secret was safe.

Glenn agreed to joint custody and moved his law practice to Illinois where Diana saw him on holidays and summer vacations. In Roberta's mind, all was perfect until the morning of Diana's seventeenth birthday when she slipped up and told Diana a half-truth about her birth father. Roberta was aware of Diana's penchant for solving mysteries, and feared she had roused Diana's curiosity. However, in her typical Roberta fashion, she dismissed the possibility of discovery and fell into a deeper sense of denial.

She crushed her cigarette into an already full ashtray and felt her stomach flip-flop as she recalled how her web of lies had unraveled when Diana reconciled fact with fiction. On her own and with Glenn's help, she discovered irrefutable facts, which resulted in civil action against Roberta. Fearing impending arrest and incarceration,

Roberta dodged them and refused to cooperate. However, months later, while recovering from a suicide attempt, Roberta broke down and told Diana the entire story.

Roberta bragged about how she had donned a nurse's uniform and posed as a member of the medical staff. She entered the nursery, snatched Diana, and smuggled her out in an oversized purse. Diana appeared so shocked by the confession, before she walked out of the hospital room, she told Roberta she would never see her again.

After their blowup, Roberta relied on Zoë for company and tried to convince herself she didn't care if she and Diana had a relationship. However, over time, she came to feel differently and desired to see, or at least talk to Diana. Roberta always felt better when she could garner attention, even if it was in bits and pieces.

She reclined on the bed and tried to sort through her conflicting emotions. Roberta was jarred back to reality when her cell phone vibrated and she saw her lawyer's number show up.

Damn, what now?

CHAPTER 7
Kevin

"HEY, MR. B, THIS IS KEVIN. Have you gotten any closer to finding the infamous Calvin and those thugs who beat me up and dumped me in Canada?"

"I've been working on your case and will present my findings to my law partner, John Bergan, later this week," Glenn said.

"I know this is awkward, with his son possibly being one of the guys we're looking for." Kevin paced back and forth in his parents' living room and fought off a recurring panic attack. "But the thugs kept calling me Calvin and asking for payment."

"I'm afraid he is the Calvin everyone's looking for. To me it looks like he was involved in a bad drug deal which forced the goons to demand money, and you were caught up in it by mistake. You and Calvin do look a lot alike."

Kevin shrugged off Glenn's comment. "What do you think will happen next?"

"My investigators will check leads and question their sources. I can't say for sure, but I predict the facts will speak for themselves, and then the shit will hit the fan."

Kevin stopped pacing; sweat ran down his forehead and he felt dizzy. "I appreciate all the work you and the Ace Detective Agency did to help bring me home. Without it who knows where I'd be or if I'd even be alive?"

Kevin suffered from PTSD and had recurring flashbacks of waking up in the Canadian hospital after the police found him unconscious and badly beaten in a rundown hotel room. The Windsor police had declared him a *John Doe*. He was presumed to be a Canadian citizen and treated for cuts, bruises, concussion, and amnesia, which required him to stay several weeks at Windsor's Regional Hospital.

"I'm glad you and Diana were friends or we'd never been able to help. It all turned out as well as if we had planned it that way," Glenn said.

"No kidding. Speaking of Diana, I have to call her. We haven't talked since yesterday."

"Tell her *Hello* from me and let her know Socks is missing her."

"Will do, sir."

Kevin hung up and headed to his car. He always felt better when he went for a drive with the windows down. It helped to clear his head and temporarily banish panic attacks. Before starting the engine, he glanced at his forearm to the tattoo of a tree trunk with his and Diana's initials. *I miss you, Di.*

CHAPTER 8
Tread Carefully

DIANA FOUND EMILY in the den leaning over the computer keyboard and squinting at the screen. "Mom, do you have a few minutes?"

"I have as much time as you want." Emily removed her reading glasses and smiled. "My eyes need a rest anyway."

Diana thought her mother had the sweetest face this side of heaven. She closed the door with a soft *click* and stood by the door, unsure of how to continue. "I was wondering if you could tell me a little more about what it was like … I mean what happened after I was stolen from you and Daddy."

Emily put her hands in her lap where they fluttered for a few seconds like a restless butterfly unsure of where to land. "It was like you had died at birth. The whole world went dark, stayed dark for months, years really." She raised her head, her lips quivered.

Diana knelt on the floor and held Emily's trembling hands. "I'm so sorry."

Emily leaned over and kissed the top of Diana's head. "It was that terrible woman's doing. We never understood why God let it happen." She took a deep breath and shuddered. "The hospital, police, and our private detectives never gave up. They checked the airlines, trains, bus stations, everywhere, but you had vanished. We simply ran out of places to look."

She raised Diana's face and held it in her hands. "It's over now and it will be good, all good from here on. We'll create *wonderful* memories." She was smiling, but she squinted as she said, "I don't want to look back."

Diana returned her mother's smile as the deep chasm of fear and loneliness began to fill and overflow with acceptance and love. She wanted to comfort her mother, but couldn't find the words. Instead, she buried her face into her mother's lap and cried pent-up tears. Emily stroked Diana's head and murmured reassuring words. With each touch, Diana felt loved. Conversely, she remembered how Roberta would give her cold stares and flippant comments. She would say, 'We'll see.' or 'I don't have time for you now, maybe later.' But Roberta rarely held true to her semi-promises. Diana looked up and smiled at her mother with tear-filled eyes.

Emily handed Diana a tissue from her pocket. "You lost your childhood and we lost our beautiful baby to a monster. We were all terribly wronged, but nothing or no one will take you from us again."

Diana leaned back on her heels and remained on the floor. "Have you got a lawyer yet, and what are you going to do about … it?"

A tap on the door interrupted them. "Come in," Emily said.

A sandy-haired head poked around the door. "Hey, Mom, wha'cha doing?" Bryan asked.

"Having some girl talk," Emily said as she brushed a tear from her eye.

"Oh." Bryan appeared embarrassed. "Wondered if I could go to Randy's house for a while. He has a new computer game."

"Yes, son. Be home by four."

His freckled face broke into a smile. "See ya'." His footfalls could be heard as he raced down the hall.

"He's cute," Diana said.

"He is indeed. Your brother is quite the character. And he can be pretty stubborn." Emily smiled.

"I've noticed. Do you think he'll ever warm up to me?"

"I do. But he's the youngest and usually gets the most attention, good and bad, depending on his behavior. I think he feels threatened, probably jealous, with you coming into his life with little warning. Give him time." She smiled. "He's a good boy."

Diana leaned forward and gave her mother a hug. "I know how it is to feel threatened and off balance. I'll be patient with him."

* * *

Glenn tapped on John Bergan's office door and entered when he heard, "Come in." John was standing with his suitcoat unbuttoned, leaning against his mahogany desk. It was almost as if he had been waiting for Glenn to show up.

"Have a few minutes?" Glenn asked.

"A few." John sounded curt.

"We need to talk about the case I'm working on. It very well could involve your son."

"I've heard scuttlebutt around the office. Do you really think *my* son is somehow involved with this kid, what's his name – Kevin – because they both happen to go to Kent State?"

"I'm saying, it's possible the bad guys and Calvin had some unfinished business and someone mistook Kevin for your son. They roughed him up, stuffed him in a van, and took him to Canada where they beat him up and left him for dead," Glenn said.

"This story is based on?"

"On my preliminary investigation, on the detectives' reports, from their interviews with witnesses who were willing to help, on ..."

John interrupted. "Really? And you're buying it? You take the word of two-bit hoods and your so-called investigators?" He dropped his arms and shoved his hands into his pockets. "What about our friendship, our partnership in this law firm?" His eyes appeared to bulge out of his sockets. His hands stretched the pocket seams close to bursting. Sweat formed on John's forehead.

Glenn was surprised to see John's renowned self-control dissolving like an antacid in a glass of water. He felt his stomach churn. "John, this isn't easy for me either. I hate even having this conversation, but ..."

"Stop." John raised his right hand. "Don't pull any courtroom stunts with me. I know them all. Hell, I wrote the script for most of them." He walked behind his desk and sharply tapped its surface with his fingertips.

"I can see this isn't going anywhere. We'll talk later." Glenn walked out and slammed the door.

He stood in the hallway and tried to gather his thoughts. *This could get messy. I hope Kevin is up for it.*

* * *

Roberta talked her way into an interview for the clerk position at Pendleton Woolen Mill's Outlet Store, but afterwards didn't feel as confident as she had after applying at the Rainbow a few weeks before.

She got back into her car, slammed the door shut, opened the window, and lit a cigarette. *It should have been a no-brainer. I can't believe I can't get a decent job in this one-horse-town.* She drummed the fingers of her free hand on the steering wheel. *What the?* She saw a familiar figure a few yards away.

"Zoë." Roberta stuck her head out the window and waved. "Over here."

Her long-time friend ran toward the car with dangly earrings bouncing against her cheek and long skirt tangling around her legs. She stopped to catch her breath and waved her hand across her face.

"When I got into town, I stopped by Irma's house and she said you were at the Mill having an interview."

"Good to see you. Get in, old girl." Roberta used her nickname for her friend, even though she knew it rankled Zoë.

Zoë hopped in and arranged her full cotton skirt neatly around her legs. "It's karma that I found you so easily." She smiled and leaned over to give Roberta a light kiss on the cheek.

"Why didn't you call first?" Roberta took another drag on her cigarette and blew the smoke out the window.

"It was a last-minute decision. I felt like taking a road trip, but didn't want to disappoint you if I had to change plans. You know I read my horoscope every day and watch the celestial signs." She rolled the window down and took a breath of fresh air.

"I'm glad you're here, but I get the feeling you're going to tell me something." Roberta threw her smoldering cigarette out the window.

Zoë shifted in her seat to look Roberta in the eyes. "Well. This guy came by a couple days ago and asked me if I was Roberta Baker. He was carrying a large envelope. It looked official. I had a feeling it was important. Were you expecting mail?" She paused. "Let me put it this way, are you in any kind of trouble?"

Roberta looked away before she responded. "It's possible. Things could get ugly real soon."

CHAPTER 9
Uncertain Futures

DIANA ANSWERED HER PHONE on the way into J. Crew at Washington Square Mall. "Hi, Cass. What's up?"

"Di, will you be in Portland middle of October, the sixteenth?"

"Pretty sure, why?"

"I'm coming to town for an interview, but not with Le Cordon Bleu College. I had it all planned out, but they're *closing* in January. At first I was majorly upset. Anyway, if I'm accepted by my second choice, the Oregon Culinary Institute, I'll start winter quarter."

Diana pumped her fist in the air. "Great. We'll get together for sure. How long will you be in town and where are you staying?"

"Not sure, two, three days. I'll probably stay in downtown Portland so I can walk to my interview. How far is that from you?"

"Not far mile-wise, but probably forty-five minutes away time-wise." Diana waved at Kate and Kerri to go ahead and start shopping and she'd catch up. "Keep me posted and we'll connect as soon as you get to town. My sisters are trying to get my attention. We're in J. Crew." Diana gave them a thumbs-up and a wait-a-minute sign.

"Well, I can't compete with shopping." Cassie laughed. "Talk to you later. And thanks, Di."

"Anytime, Cass."

* * *

Emily and Diana were in the kitchen washing dishes after breakfast the next morning. Emily put down the dish towel. "Diana, let's talk." She sat on a barstool and patted the empty one.

"What's wrong?" Diana hiccupped.

"I don't mean to sound mysterious, but we haven't talked about your grandparents. They're anxious to meet you."

Diana set down the stack of clean dishes. "I wondered if they were still alive."

"Yes, my parents, Sam and Louise, live in Vancouver, Washington and James' parents, Richard and Rachel, are in San Francisco. However, Mama is living in an assisted living facility. She was diagnosed with Alzheimer's three years ago."

"Oh, I'm sorry. How sad."

"It's been hard on everyone. Mama's getting worse and … we don't want to wait any longer to get you together." Emily cleared her throat. "Sweetheart, she was my strength, my rock, the one who urged me to keep going after you were taken from us. You see, I was numbed-out on medication, curled up in a ball, and didn't get out of bed for weeks. Your father was panic-stricken and decided to take time off work, but Mama and Daddy moved in to help. She cooked, cleaned, and nursed me back to health. Daddy stayed by James every step of the way." She smiled. "They did *guy* things. If they hadn't been so loving and generous, I don't know if our marriage would have survived. Or if I would have survived."

Diana reached over to hold her mother's hand. Emily nodded. "Mama understood. She had lost several babies to miscarriages. I'm their only child and was born the year she turned forty. When you were stolen, she did the only thing she knew best. I wanted to do the same for her when she fell ill, but your grandpa said, 'No.' He didn't want to upset our family life."

Diana's eyes filled with tears. "Gosh. I can't wait to see them."

Emily patted Diana's hand and got up. "Good. We'll do it this Saturday. I've been praying for the right time. I've prepared Mama."

Diana thought her mother looked wistful when she said, "I think Mama's eyes lit up when I told her about you." She held up her forefinger. "But, she thinks of you as Julia Louise, which is your given name."

"I know. I saw my birth certificate."

"We haven't decided how to introduce you. I think taking it moment by moment is the best." Emily smiled. "Let's go out for coffee since the rest of the gang is at school and work. Where's your favorite place?"

"Starbucks."

* * *

Diana stood outside the door of her grandmother's apartment at Columbia Crest and reached for her mother's hand. Diana felt her mother gently squeeze hers in return. She saw Grandma Louise sitting in a chair by the window. Her silver hair shone in the sunlight and she possessed a serene beauty that belied her age and declining health. Her grandmother's eyes were closed and her delicate hands rested in her lap as if in prayer; however, she opened her eyes when Diana, Emily, and James entered the room.

"Mama, you're looking well today," Emily said. Louise's face crinkled into a smile and her blue eyes sparkled. "We brought you a special visitor."

Diana let go of her mother's hand and stepped forward. "Hello, Grandma." She felt her throat tighten; she fought off tears and the urge to hiccup. "It's me, Julia Louise, your granddaughter."

James put his arm around his wife's shoulder; she snuggled into his chest as tears rolled down her cheeks.

"My, my, it's so nice to see you again. How you've grown." Louise moved as if to stand.

"Don't get up, Grandma. I'll pull a chair over." Diana sat across and took her grandmother's hands in hers. Diana leaned forward and their heads almost touched while they talked and giggled like two schoolgirls.

The family kept the visit to a half-hour so as not to tire Louise. Diana was reluctant to leave; when James, Emily, and Diana stood in the lobby to re-group, she asked, "Grandma remembers me. But how?"

"The brain is a funny thing. Even with Alzheimer's she must remember your birth, but not your disappearance. You've been alive in her heart and mind and the past has caught up with the present," Emily said.

"She's sweet and so beautiful. I wish I'd known her before." Diana sniffled.

"Here you go. I always bring a handful of tissues when we visit." Emily handed her two.

They went to the parking lot where the three stood with heads bowed and arms around each other's waists. James led them in prayer. "We are so blessed and grateful for Louise, it's like nothing ever happened."

"Now, if only Mama could remember what day it is and who *I* am," Emily said.

* * *

Roberta and Zoë sat in Irma's kitchen drinking coffee late in the afternoon. Golden rays shining through the kitchen window bounced off the white countertop, but didn't lighten Roberta's dark mood. *Holy crap, this is all I need, being hounded by lawyers.* She was on her third cigarette even though Irma had asked her to quit smoking in the house. Irma was working night shift and Roberta had plenty of time to air out the house.

"I hate to be the bearer of bad news, but as your friend and psychic advisor, I wanted to tell you about the envelope in person." Zoë twisted her beaded necklace around her long fingers accented with colorful manicured nails.

Roberta took a protracted drag on her cigarette and held it for a few seconds before she blew it across the table. "It's not your fault. All I wanted to do was get on with life and not have to put up with crap from *anyone*."

"I don't know the details, but I can see your aura is disturbed. It isn't healthy, my dear."

Roberta waved her hands over her head. "Aura-schmora. I have bigger troubles. Diana has no conscience *or* character and won't let bygones be bygones."

"I'm sorry you and your daughter are having problems. I wish there was something I could do to help." She sipped her cold coffee and made a face. Her eyes brightened. "Is there?"

Roberta shook her head. "Not now. But I might have to blow this town and move back to Boise. The job isn't working out and Irma's been making noises about my moving out. I have to get ahold of my attorney ASAP."

"Attorney? As serious as that?"

"Hell yes, it's serious. This could get nasty real fast, but I won't take it lying down." Roberta thumped the table with her forefinger. "I can kick butt with the best of them."

Zoë stood, walked to the sink, and rinsed her cup. "Roberta, maybe we should have a tarot card reading. I always have them with me."

Roberta scoffed. "Think it'll help?"

"Yes, dear, it always helps. Let's clear the table. Does your friend have a tablecloth? The darker the color, the better."

"I don't know," Roberta snapped.

Zoë put her hands on her hips. "Could you check, please? I need a semblance of atmosphere." She waved her hands toward the window. "And we must close the curtains. I can't make a proper connection with all this light streaming in. It disturbs your natural aura." She pointed to the candles on the shelf above the table. "Do you think Irma would mind if I use these?"

Roberta glanced over her shoulder while she rummaged through drawers. "They're probably thrift shop. Dime a dozen."

Zoë inspected the candles. "They're a little worse for wear, but should do the trick."

"This is all I could find, but it's more like an oversized placemat." Roberta held up an oval-shaped cloth and gave it a good shake. Dust motes floated in the sunlight.

Zoë inspected the placemat. "This will work fine. I need something soft to set my cards on. Close the curtains, please." She fingered her necklace. "Now, may I have a match?"

Roberta retrieved her cigarette lighter from her jeans' pocket and handed it to Zoë. Then Zoë placed the candles in a semi-circle on the opposite end of the table, closed her eyes for a moment, and lit them. She arranged the meager cloth in the center of the table and patted down the frayed edges. Zoë took the tarot cards from her skirt pocket and removed them from a black silk hanky.

Roberta was familiar with the cards which were twice the size of playing cards and imprinted with mystical characters and symbols: knights and ladies, dragons and castles, a hooded figure holding a scythe, the earth, moon, stars, and symbol for fire.

Zoë set the well-used cards on their edge and shuffled them with the expertise of a Las Vegas card dealer. She waved at the empty chair. "Please sit and then cut the cards. It's always best you touch them before I begin." Zoë inhaled the scent from the candles. "Vanilla, umm, calming."

Roberta slid into her chair and waited. Zoë dealt out the first row. She shook her head and made a clucking sound.

"What's wrong?" Roberta leaned forward.

"I don't like the looks of this. See the knight waving his sword over his head?"

Roberta nodded.

"I see conflict with a man, a tall man." She tapped her long fingernail on the second card depicting a lady. "Could this be your daughter?"

"This is a re-hash of previous readings. Can't you come up with new material?" Roberta leaned back and kicked the table leg.

"The cards are a guide. I use them to see the present and the future." Zoë swept her arms in an outward motion. "Then it's up to you to find the answers that best suit your circumstances. There is a pattern here." She touched the knight. "I cannot change the inevitable. It is what it is." She flipped over another card and revealed a castle. "This indicates you will be moving soon."

Roberta snorted. "I've told you I'm going to leave this one-horse-town. As you can see, Irma's place sure isn't a castle."

Zoë leaned back. "Roberta, I must work in an atmosphere of trust and without the sarcasm. We've had this discussion before. Do you want my help or not?"

"Yes, yes. I'm having a bad day." Roberta waved her hand in frustration. "Go on."

"I don't mean to sound pushy, Roberta, but I have to return to Boise tomorrow. I'm leading a psychic advisor's training session at the Community Center on Wednesday evening."

"Glad to hear Boise will have its fair share of fortune tellers." Zoë winced at the term fortune teller as she took Roberta's hand.

Roberta leaned forward and forced herself to listen without further comments.

* * *

On Sunday evening, James and Emily asked Diana to join them in the living room. James stood in front of the fireplace; Diana and Emily sat on the couch. "Sweetheart, it's time we catch you up on a few things. Ever since we'd heard you had been found, your mother and I have been considering what to do next. We want to do the right thing, both legally and ethically."

He put his hands in his pockets and paced. "It isn't right to let that woman get away with abducting you, fleeing the state, preventing us from raising you, loving you." He paused and wiped his eyes with the back of his hand. "But most of all, she stole your rightful childhood and usurped our lives on every level." He pounded the mantelpiece and rattled a vase. "She broke all of our hearts."

"Yes, and we also wonder what *else* she's done or what she might still do," Emily said.

"Precisely. We consulted our lawyer who then contacted the District Attorney. We had to know where we stood in regards to filing a criminal or civil lawsuit."

"Oh." Diana hiccupped.

"We've been told we can file a civil and a criminal case. Do you know the difference?" James asked.

"Kind of. One means jail and the other is about money," Diana said.

James nodded. "Close enough. If we file a civil lawsuit against Roberta, specifically for emotional damages and pain and suffering, it's about financial compensation. We probably won't see a dime; however, it would send a strong message her crime won't be ignored. A criminal lawsuit would be another story. It would get real nasty, not to mention the stress and publicity. If we win, she'll go to jail."

"I see." Diana looked at her mother.

"I know. This is hard to hear, but there has to be consequences for such a terrible crime," Emily said.

"For me, I can't wait to look her in the eye and tell her what kind of person I think she is." James ended his tirade and sat in the leather chair by the fireplace. He leaned forward and looked at Diana.

"You don't know Mama, I mean Roberta." Diana blushed. "She's tough and mean, and will probably yell and call you names, even in front of the judge."

"Well, I can take it." James gave a wry chuckle.

Diana massaged her abdomen. "I'm okay with whatever you decide. There were so many times growing up when I wanted to tell her how mean she'd been and how bad she made me feel." Diana brushed a lock of hair from her sweaty forehead. "But I guess I kind of did when I moved in with Cassie and her mother to finish my senior year. Roberta was so mad, she called me names, grabbed my arm, and twisted it hard." She rubbed her wrist. "But I'd still hate to see her go to jail."

James leaned back in the chair. "You've told us how you feel about this; however, the matter may be out of our hands. I'll call our attorney in the morning."

Emily drew Diana to her breast and gave her a hug. "We can't let her get away with her terrible crime." She lifted Diana's chin to look into her daughter's eyes. "You understand, don't you?"

"An eye for an eye," Diana whispered.

CHAPTER 10
Legal Moves

GLENN AND HIS LAW PARTNER, John Bergan, agreed to meet again to discuss the sensitive case involving Glenn's client, Kevin and John's son, Calvin. Their previous spontaneous and hostile conversation had been a waste of time, and Glenn felt badly about bringing it up when he did. However, he believed it was right to discuss the progress of his investigation into Kevin's abduction with John. Maybe Calvin wasn't involved, maybe his detectives were on a wild-goose chase, either way Glenn wanted to talk to John's son.

Glenn stood at the picture window and watched the last of the red leaves falling from the giant maples, which were purportedly planted by settlers in the mid-nineteenth century. *I used to think my office had the best view in the building, especially in October.* He shook his head. *Today, I'm not feeling it. Not one bit.*

He turned at the sound of the door opening. His law partner strode across the room without a word, yanked out a client chair, and sat. John appeared to wait for Glenn to make the first move.

"Thank you for coming. Like a cup of coffee?" John shook his head. "I need one." Glenn poured a cup from the silver carafe and stirred in a few drops of half-and-half. He sat behind his desk and played with the plastic spoon. "So, here we are again."

John leaned back in his chair. "What next?"

"Well that's the sixty-four-thousand-dollar question." Glenn cleared his throat. "I need to get to the *who* and *why* behind the attack on Kevin Wright last spring. Calvin might be able to shed some light on it."

"I repeat. I don't see how."

"John, the police were called in immediately and after weeks of investigating were unable to find Kevin or any trail his abductors might have left. However, my detectives have discovered solid evidence of a drug ring, likely operating from one of the fraternities, and unfortunately Calvin's name came up more than once."

"Bull."

"I have to pursue every possibility; however, I can only imagine what you're feeling if Calvin is involved."

John pounded his fist on the desk. "You have no idea what I'm feeling. If you did we wouldn't be having this conversation."

"I should have phrased it better. Kevin is a close friend of the family and I've been asked to carry their inquiry forward. He was abducted, beaten, taken into Canada, and left for dead. As I said, at the time, the police investigated on both sides of the border, but without results, so his parents hired me. They want answers, hell, I want answers. The police have been updated and are working on their end. It's going to be rough, but I have to follow any leads to find the perpetrators and bring them to justice," Glenn concluded.

"Do what you think is necessary, but I'm not letting my son talk to you or your so-called investigators." John headed to the door and held the door handle for a moment. He spoke to the floor, "I assume this conspiracy story isn't common knowledge."

"So far it's between you, Kevin, and my investigatory team; however, a couple of people in the office know. That couldn't be helped, I'm afraid."

John left without another word.

"Fine, we'll do it without your cooperation." Glenn pulled his office phone closer and dialed a number he used only in emergencies.

* * *

Roberta finished her morning shift at the Rainbow and then sat at the counter with a half cup of coffee and a doughnut. She craved a cigarette, but held off going into the alley for a smoke break. "Good to see you again, how's it going?" A regular customer waved to her as he headed toward the front door.

"Great," Roberta said. *Right. Just great. I can't seem to start over, can't find a decent job.* She stared into the mirror behind the counter and saw the reflection of the giant buffalo head hanging on the opposite wall above the row of booths. *I hate that thing.*

She gripped her long black braid and played with the rubber band at its end. *Time to call Charles for some advice.* She pushed her cup toward the edge of the counter and waved to Sadie for a refill. *Why can't Diana forget the past and let me get on with my life? Her parents must be pushing the lawsuit.* A chill went down her spine. *And the police could be hot on my trail.*

Sadie's question broke Roberta's train of miserable thoughts. "Can you work a split-shift today? Gloria called in sick. Her kid's home from school. Something about him having a bad cold."

"Yeah, sure. Got nothing else to do." Roberta snorted. "What a wuss. Staying home because of a cold. My kid was tougher than that." Roberta watched Sadie roll her eyes in apparent disgust. "What?"

"Nothing. None of my business."

"Damn straight."

* * *

Roberta leaned against the cement wall in the alley behind the café, lit a cigarette, and called her lawyer. "This is Roberta Baker. I need to talk to Charles."

"I'll make sure he gets your message and he'll call you back before the end of the day," Charles Carson's legal assistant said.

"Tell him who it is. He'll take my call."

"But ..."

"Just *do* it." She was put on hold. Roberta kicked a pop can across the asphalt and threw her cigarette on the gravel next to the dumpster. After a couple of minutes, she heard a man's voice.

His opening was blunt. "Berta, who the hell do you think you are talking to my secretary like that? Believe it or not, you are *not* my only client."

Roberta paced up and down the alley. "It's an *emergency*. I think a process server showed up in Boise, where I'd been living. How in the hell did they find me?"

Charles emitted an exaggerated sigh. "You can run, but you can't hide."

Roberta grimaced. "My friend who lives in Boise told me some guy showed up at her house asking for me. He had a large envelope, and he sure as hell wasn't UPS."

"I was afraid of this."

"We've been through this before. *Remember?*"

"Where are you now? I heard rumors you left town in a hurry."

"Rumors, from who?" Charles didn't reply. "I'm in a hick town in eastern Oregon. Ever heard of Pendleton?"

"Yes." Charles sounded irritated.

"Don't be so snippy," Roberta said.

"Is this a temporary living arrangement?"

"Totally. But I haven't figured out for how long."

"You shouldn't have left Idaho in the first place. It doesn't look good." He paused. "Okay, come to my office Tuesday afternoon."

"That's tomorrow!"

"So, when can I expect you?" Charles sounded sarcastic.

"I'll be there Wednesday morning and I want you to help me come up with a plan."

Roberta didn't wait for a response; she hung up and stormed back to the café to take the afternoon shift.

CHAPTER 11
Cooking Up Plans

CASSIE WOKE AT 6 A.M. to her phone alarm. She had slept well despite being alone in a downtown Portland hotel room. She swung out of bed, walked to the window, and looked onto the empty street where the streetlights were winking, signaling they were ready to shut down. She stretched her arms up, drew a deep breath, held it for a few seconds, and let it out. *No time for yoga this morning.*

Cassie spent extra time dressing, fixing her hair, and applying her makeup for the most important day in her life, career-wise. She had her favorite beverage and breakfast sandwich at the corner Starbucks and walked six blocks uptown to the culinary school. It was a modern building with a gleaming white tile floor. Her high heels clicked as she hurried across the lobby. She entered the first office door and stepped up to the desk where Robin, the administrative assistant, looked up and smiled.

"How may I help you?" Robin asked.

"I'm Cassie Thomas and I have an appointment today. I'm scheduled for an interview and an entrance exam." She tried to sound controlled and professional, but her heart pounded like a jackhammer. Her feet throbbed from the long walk on the concrete pavement in heels.

"Yes. Have a seat and I'll get your paperwork," Robin said as she scooted her chair back, stood, and flipped her hand through a row of manila folders in the file cabinet. She handed the paperwork and a clipboard to Cassie. "Please take a seat over there and fill out the forms." She waved to a row of cushioned chairs against the wall.

After Cassie handed in the forms, Robin asked a teammate to cover her desk while she took Cassie on a quick tour of the kitchens, classrooms, and the common area where students gathered on their breaks. Robin ended the tour at the exam room on the second floor.

Robin opened the door a crack and pointed inside. Cassie saw several rows of computers situated on long desks. She noticed translucent white shades covering the windows, letting in the morning sun, and giving the room a cheerful atmosphere. "As you can see, the exam will be taken online, so pick a chair," Robin said. "The exam begins in twenty minutes."

"How many will take the test?" Cassie asked.

"You are one of five candidates today. We don't test any less than five at a time." She smiled. "When the proctor says, "Time's up," save your work and close the program. I will post the scores online this afternoon, but you may call me if you prefer. Any questions?"

"No, but I'm surprised the results will be available so soon."

"The answers are pretty cut and dried." Robin chuckled. "Sorry for the pun." Cassie smiled politely. "Anyway, good luck. The test will take ninety minutes. I have scheduled your interview for 11:30."

"Thank you." Cassie was so nervous she didn't know what else to say. She watched Robin walk away and entered the room where one candidate sat in the last row. Cassie smiled at the young man, who nodded at her, and quickly redirected his attention to his phone. Cassie took a seat near the front and tried to calm her nerves by counting backwards from one hundred.

* * *

Diana waited until two o'clock before she called Cassie. "Okay, you've kept me in suspense long enough. How did the test and interview go?"

Cassie sounded out of breath when she answered her phone. "I had my interview during lunch, so I had to grab something from a street vendor afterwards. Have you tried the street tacos?"

"No, and I don't care about tacos. I want to know how it went." Diana couldn't wait for Cassie to get to the point.

"I checked online a few minutes ago. I scored ninety percent on the written exam, and I must have done well during my interview, because I begin cooking classes in January. Can you believe it?"

"Yes, and it's the best news I've heard all week." Diana picked up an orange from the fruit bowl and rolled it around on the counter. "Have you thought about where you're going to live?"

"No. This hasn't hit me yet. Maybe you can help me out."

"Don't worry, we'll research it together. I'll ask Mom if I can borrow the car and we can go for coffee and a snack. Where are you exactly?" Diana listened carefully and took notes on an envelope. "I'll be there in a half hour, maybe forty-five minutes depending on traffic."

"I'll wait in the courtyard out front. You can drive right up, no problem. I'm too excited to go back to my hotel room and I might get lost if I stray too far. Portland is way bigger than little-ol' Boise." Cassie chuckled.

Diana held up one finger and mouthed, *Just a minute*, when Emily entered the kitchen. "Sounds like a plan, Cassie, but if I can't borrow the car, I'll call you right back." She hung up and set her phone on the counter.

"I didn't mean to interrupt," Emily said.

"You didn't. Cass had her test and interview at the culinary school today and she made the cut. She'll be a Portlander in a few weeks."

"Wonderful. I'm so glad you'll have Cassie living close by. She can help you adjust. I know you get along with the twins, but you need a friend your own age."

"We've known each other like forever, and it will be great having her here." Diana stood. "May I borrow your car? I'd like to pick her up."

"Certainly." Emily got the keys from her purse. "Here you are." Emily brushed her daughter's cheek with a kiss. "Drive carefully, sweetheart."

Diana felt herself blush with gratitude. She was still getting used to having a parent who expressed her positive, loving feelings so generously. "Thanks, Mom. Cassie and I will go out for coffee after and come back. I hate to leave Cassie at the hotel by herself. Do you mind an extra person for dinner?"

"Not in the least. I'd be disappointed if you didn't invite her. I'm looking forward to meeting Cassie, the future famous chef."

"I'll tell her that her fan club awaits." Diana laughed.

* * *

Roberta called Zoë after she finished packing her suitcase with enough things for a week. "I'm heading out tomorrow and will be in Boise by five. Is my room in one piece or do I need to get a hotel?"

"No need for that. Your room is just like you left it. It will be nice to have you back."

"I knew I could count on you." Roberta took a long drag on her cigarette and held her breath longer than usual before she exhaled. "I'm not moving back for good. It will be just long enough for me and my lawyer to straighten out a few things."

After a beat or two, Zoë said, "I see. Drive safely. If I'm not home, the key will be under the pot with the pink geranium. And then I'd like to find out what's troubling you, my friend."

"We'll see." Roberta fell back on a non-committal response. She hung up, went to the kitchen, and sat at the table. She watched Irma prepare dinner and, as usual, didn't offer to help. "I have a couple of appointments in Boise. I'll be leaving tomorrow and will be gone for a few days."

Irma stopped stirring the stew. On the wall above the stove, the vintage black and white cat clock's tail swayed in time with its oversized eyes. Roberta thought it appeared interested in their conversation.

"I hope it's nothing serious," Irma said.

"No, nothing to worry about." Roberta glanced up. "Those cat eyes give me the creeps the way they move back and forth. Like it's alive." She shuddered. "I told Sadie I'd be back for the dinner shift next Friday."

"Things have slowed down since the Rodeo ended last month. The Rainbow can do fine without you, I'm sure." Irma tapped the spoon on the edge of the pot and set it on the counter.

"They'll survive all right. In fact, this whole town would get along just fine without me."

"You're not happy here, are you?" Irma switched the unit to low and joined Roberta whose jittery leg was jarring the table leg and making it sway.

"Not really, but who can say what happiness is?"

"I believe if we think good thoughts, good things will happen."

"Huh, well maybe your life is all tied up with a neat little bow, but mine sure as hell isn't." Roberta was getting frustrated with Irma's Pollyanna attitude.

Irma leaned forward. "Even so, think positive and appreciate what God has given you and things will surely take a turn for the better."

"Do you have everything you want? Are *you* happy?"

Irma gazed to the middle of her kitchen table and smiled at the antique vase holding a silk flower arrangement. "See that vase?" Roberta nodded. "It's one of the few things my mother left me.

When I look at it, I think of her and I'm happy." She leaned forward. "Roberta, it's usually the little things that count."

Roberta frowned. "I'm not so sure … I have big problems, and a bunch of flowers can't make me feel better."

Irma smiled and patted Roberta's hand. "I wish I could help you feel better about yourself and the current situation. But how you approach life must come from within." She patted her chest. "When you return, how about attending church with me?"

Roberta's eyebrows arched. "Church? I'd rather chew on ground glass."

Irma scowled. "I'm sorry you feel that way. But if you ever feel differently, the invitation is always open."

She returned to the stove, checked the stew, and opened the oven door. "The rolls are done. Could you get me a plate?"

The homey scent of baked bread filled the kitchen and despite her foul mood, Roberta felt better.

*   *   *

Diana picked Cassie up in front of the Oregon Culinary Institute and then headed downtown in search of an on-street parking spot. "Here's one. Thank gosh it's on the corner, so I won't have to parallel park," Diana said. "It should only be a few short blocks to your Starbucks."

"My Starbucks. That's funny."

They walked four blocks and entered the busy café. "There's two chairs. I'll put my bag down. Can I have your jacket so I can save the other one?" Diana asked.

After receiving their order, they sat in oversized leather chairs by the front window. "I was wondering when you choose a place to live, if you could get an apartment big enough for two," Diana asked.

Cassie set her Danish on the plate and wiped her lips and fingers. "Two? You and me? Super, but what about your family?"

Diana twirled a lock of her hair. "I'm getting restless. The twins are back in school; Mom and I have too much time on our hands and Bryan is a pain. I can't be sure, but I think he's taking things from my room." She leaned back and sighed. "Anyway, I've been thinking about getting my car and signing up for classes at Portland Community College."

Cassie sat back and tucked both feet beneath her. "Sounds like you have this planned out."

"You're looking at me kind of funny."

Cassie unwrinkled her nose. "I didn't mean to. I'm just trying to figure things out. Can you afford to share an apartment? And how do you think your parents will take the news?"

Diana sighed. "Don't get me wrong, it's great having my family, a dream come true, but … I feel uncomfortable. Except for The Pain, they are sweet, too sweet. It's like being smothered in chocolate fudge and whipped cream. I need some space."

"As far as money, I plan on getting a part-time job at Starbucks or maybe a restaurant. That way I can work evenings and weekends. I have savings. Dad started a college fund when I was a baby, so tuition won't be a problem."

Cassie nodded. "But I don't get why you don't move back home. I mean, back to Illinois and Glenn. Kevin must be going crazy with you clear out here."

"I've thought about it, but the time isn't right." Diana waved her arms around. "There are so many places I want to see. I was born in Portland, but was cheated out of all of it." She raised her voice. "I haven't been *anywhere*, except to Neskowin last month with my folks, and to Astoria. Remember when Kev and Big Stan and I followed Roberta there last summer and we had a showdown?"

Cassie patted Diana's arm. "Shhh, people are looking."

"Sorry." Diana sipped her coffee. "Anyway, I need my Buffy Bug so I can hit the road and just drive. I want the feeling I had when I ran on the beach with my sisters. It felt so good to let loose and feel the wind in my face."

"Speaking of face, you have a mocha mustache." Diana pointed to Cassie's upper lip.

Cassie took her napkin and wiped off the light brown mustache left from her café mocha. "I get it. You gotta do your thing. That's why I didn't sign up for regular college. It would have been a huge mistake and I'd have been in *way* over my head, not smothered, but drowned. Cooking school is the perfect place for me." Cassie leaned over and squeezed Diana's hand.

"See, you know who you *are* and I'm still trying to figure myself out. I'm eighteen and just found my birth family." Diana paused. "The last thing Dad said was how much he wants me to go to college. I hate to admit he's right, but everyone knows how much I love school and how badly I want to teach."

"Totally. You're really smart. Kids would love to have you as their teacher. I *might* be able to show them how to boil water." Cassie flashed her thousand-watt smile. "Want another muffin? I know how stress makes you hungry."

"Not now. And don't put yourself down," Diana said.

"What about all the legal stuff with Roberta?"

"It's up to the lawyers and most likely the police. That's another reason I have to stick around. They'll need me if it goes to trial."

"You can always fly back for meetings and stuff."

"Sure I can, but I want to stay here for now, maybe forever."

Cassie took another bite of her pastry and held it in the air momentarily. "I get it. You want to start over."

Diana nodded and stifled a hiccup.

"You're lucky, Di. You have everyone and everything on your side. You're not alone and scared to death like Roberta probably is."

"No matter how much I try to hate her, I wonder what made her steal me from my parents. It's not normal to walk into a hospital nursery and take someone else's baby."

"No kidding. So what next. I mean tonight?"

"How about coming to my house and having dinner?"

"Love to."

"And maybe stay the night. Will it be too late to check out of your hotel?"

"Not a problem, Di. It's just down the street."

Diana's phone chimed a tone she hadn't heard in several months. She looked at the caller ID and saw it was Roberta's number. "Crap. This can't be good."

CHAPTER 12
Calling in Help

GLENN WAS READY TO CALL in Big Stan: the man who had located Kevin in Canada and then prevented a disastrous showdown between Roberta and Diana in Astoria a few weeks later. An enigma, he was quiet, methodical, mysterious, and ninety-five percent successful at unraveling cold cases, bringing in the bad guys, and handling every assignment with relentless dedication.

"Stan, I need you to delve deeper into Kevin's case. I think my law partner's son's possible involvement with college campus drug deals might have led to Kevin's kidnapping."

"I had a feeling you'd be asking me to look into that further. Give me what you have and I'll get on it." His voiced sounded even-toned, steady. Glenn could count on Stan to handle sensitive matters in a professional manner.

"Let's meet at the diner on Beech Street and I'll hand over a copy of my file."

"Yes, sir. Name the time." The line went silent for a moment. "If I may ask, how's your daughter doin'? Is she happy, safe?"

"Diana is in Portland with her birth family, getting acclimated, and stretching her wings. I'd say considering everything that's happened over the last year and a half, yes, she's doing well. Thanks for asking." Glenn walked to his office window and scanned the skyline for a moment. "Stan, another thing; my practice will be going through major changes and I'd like to hire you on full time. You can have an office in the building if you wish."

"What about the Ace Detective Agency?" Stan asked.

"I'll use them, too, but I'd like you to be my principal go-to guy," Glenn said. "See you tomorrow at one, Stan."

"Sounds good."

Glenn heard a click, smiled, and set his phone on the desk. He opened a drawer and removed an envelope. He put it in his briefcase and locked it. *Just in case.*

* * *

"Calvin, get back to me as soon as you get this message. We have to talk." John hung up, stood at the picture window, and watched the setting sun spread deep purple shadows over the neighborhood. He sat at his desk and let the room go dark; with only the computer monitor as light, he loosened his tie and reached into the lower desk drawer to remove a silver flask. He blew a thin layer of dust off before he raised it to his lips.

He swallowed a third of its contents in one mouthful. The whiskey hit his esophagus and sent him into a coughing fit. He grasped his throat and reached for the water carafe to take a few sips. When his head cleared, he thought, *This can't be happening.*

Ever since his altercation with Glenn, John hadn't had a good night's sleep. He couldn't shake the feeling Glenn was onto something and the possibility his son could be involved with illegal activities, especially drugs, was too terrible to imagine.

John was a proud descendent of immigrants who came from Europe in the mid-1600s; these people subsequently held positions of power and influence in the private and public sectors for centuries. He married a woman whose family enjoyed an equal if not higher standing in their community. The thought Calvin might not follow in his footsteps as a lawyer or, worse, ruin their established reputation was totally unacceptable.

The effects of alcohol exaggerated his morose mood; he couldn't remember feeling this vulnerable, in danger of losing everything. As a lawyer, he saw needy people from all walks of life, and over the years he developed a mindset to not let toxic people affect him or his family. But he sensed the situation surrounding Calvin was evolving into a disaster. *By God, son, we will work this out. We have no other choice.* He put his face in his hands and for the second time in his life, he cried.

* * *

"Hello, Mama, uh, Roberta." Diana held her breath, sucked in her stomach, and prepared for the worst.

Roberta chuckled. "Yes, it's me young lady. I think it's time we had a chat."

"What about?"

"How about you tell your parents to call off the goons and ditch the legal moves?"

Diana choked back hiccups. "I haven't done anything. Honest. I don't want to make trouble."

"Really? Then why did a little man come to my door in Boise with a packet of official papers?"

"I don't know."

"Well, I think you do and let me tell you this, whatever you or your pretty little family are planning it won't work."

"But ..."

"You think you're so smart. Well, I've been around the block and won't be pushed into a legal mess. I can get tough, too."

The line went dead. Diana set her phone on the armrest and sighed. "Was that Roberta?" Cassie asked.

Diana nodded. She felt tears welling in her eyes and wiped them with a napkin. "Yeah. And she's really mad. She ..."

"Did she threaten you?"

"Kind of. But I don't think she'd really do anything to *me*. What can she do?"

"Make your life a living hell. Oh, Di." Cassie leaned over and gave her a hug. She released Diana and grabbed a napkin to wipe her tearing eyes.

"It isn't fair. How can such a horrible person blame me and my parents for the things *she* did?"

"Because she doesn't care about anyone but herself. I think I should drive you home."

"Sure."

* * *

Emily stopped her preparations for dinner and joined her husband in the living room. "James, I have a funny feeling about Diana."

He had begun his nightly routine of channel surfing and checking out the advertising competition. He shut off the television. "Like what?"

"I can't say exactly."

"Then give her a call." He handed her his cell phone.

Emily quickly pressed the buttons. "Hello, Diana, where are you? Are you alright?"

"I'm good, on my way home. Cassie and I are looking forward to dinner."

"I had a feeling you were in trouble or upset." Emily put her hand to her chest and tried to calm her breathing.

"Roberta just called and she's pretty mad. But I can handle it. She's the one who should be worried."

"Diana, you are not alone anymore. We'll get through this with that awful woman."

"See you soon, Mom."

Diana's stomach churned. It wasn't the first time Roberta had made her feel ill. "That was weird, Mom calling me like that."

"It is. What did she want?"

"She called because she had a feeling I was upset." Diana wasn't sure how to clarify her thoughts. "That's what I was getting at earlier, you know, about feeling smothered. I'm not used to having a mother who thinks and cares about me night and day."

"You shouldn't complain, you know." Cassie chuckled.

"I do sound kind of ungrateful." Diana blinked rapidly to keep from tearing up. "I'm not. But growing up with Roberta I learned to be on my own. You know?" Cassie nodded. "And then I spent most of last summer with Dad and saw how the other side works. He was supportive, but gave me space. Now I have a whole family: two dads, a really great mother, a brother and two sisters. How lucky can one girl be?"

"Don't forget you have a best friend."

Diana smiled. "Oh, there, take the next exit or we'll be all turned around." Her phone rang; she saw Kevin's ID, but let it go to voicemail.

Diana gazed out the window and tried to put her jumbled feelings into thoughts. *Why don't I feel the same about Kevin anymore? How could I have changed my mind about our relationship after I got to Portland? Maybe I never really loved him. Maybe I'm worried Roberta will come in and mess up my life again. It's like everything is going under water.*

She shuddered and almost blurted what she was thinking, but thought better of it. Better not distract her or we'll get in an accident. She tried to smile. *Why can't I be lighthearted like Cassie and take each day as it comes?*

CHAPTER 13
Love Pangs

KEVIN SAT ALONE on a saggy couch in the far corner of the student lounge and struggled to understand why Diana hadn't answered his messages. Was she too busy with her family or was she avoiding him? He felt another wave of nausea wash over as he made the call. As usual, Diana didn't answer so he left a voicemail. "Diana, we need to talk."

A deep voice interrupted Kevin's thoughts. "Hey, Kev, going to the library? It's getting late." Kevin looked up and saw a member of his study group.

"I'll be heading over soon. Give me fifteen minutes." Kevin smiled and gave a thumbs-up before Al disappeared around the corner. He knew he should be grateful to Glenn for suggesting a pre-law curriculum; however, projects were piling up and he was falling behind in all his classes. The goal of becoming a lawyer, joining a reputable law firm, and marrying Diana was the future he had imagined. But now he wasn't sure of anything.

Kevin packed up his books and strode across campus enveloped in oppressive thoughts reminiscent of the days he was known as

John Doe in a Canadian hospital. His head trauma had left him without memories of who he was or how he was injured. The effects lingered for several months, and he struggled with flashbacks and headaches. His physician had told him to schedule follow-up appointments if he regressed. But now nothing mattered but Diana. *I may be losing her.*

His cell rang and he hurriedly answered, "Diana?"

"No, it's Glenn."

"Oh."

"Sorry. I'll only be a minute. I've contacted Big Stan and we're meeting tomorrow to talk about the next stage. With him onboard, things should move right along." Kevin listened carefully and swallowed to rid the lump in his throat.

Glenn continued, "Then I can decide how to proceed with your case. You must be anxious to put this behind you."

"Yes, sir, I am."

"How are your studies going?"

"I'm heading to the library to work on a project right now."

"Well, I'll let you go. Give my love to Diana when you talk."

"Will do, sir. Goodbye." The autumn breeze blew dry leaves across his path; he counted them: five. Odd number. That was how he felt, odd. He tossed his backpack onto the grass and sat on a cold cement bench under a maple tree; he leaned back and looked through the web of bare branches to see the darkening sky and the first evening star winking down. His mouth formed a grim smile. *Star light, star bright, first star I see tonight. I wish Diana and I will be together forever.*

*   *   *

At dinner, Diana was happy to see Cassie looking comfortable interacting with her family. She had won them over with her endearing and slightly off-beat personality and helped raise Diana's spirits. After the dishes were cleared and loaded into the dishwasher, the twins found a decades' old Monopoly game in the closet and set it up in the family room. "This'll be fun," Kate said. "Beware, Cassie, Kerri may take all your money. She's tough."

"We'll see." Cassie blew on her hands and rubbed them together. "I'm no wuss."

Diana's heart palpitations had subsided during dessert; however, between turns throwing dice and moving her miniature shoe around the game board, she couldn't concentrate. Kevin's voicemail spoke to her conscience. She knew she had to call him back, but didn't know what to say. How does one tell an almost-fiancé the blush of first love had faded and she needed to step back? Would it push him over the edge, cause a relapse? She rotated her shoulders to loosen up. *I'm a terrible person, selfish, mixed up. As mean as Roberta?*

"Di, it's your move." Cassie nudged her.

"Oh, sorry."

"Thinking about Kevin?" Kerri teased.

"I guess I was." Diana passed GO and collected $200. Her phone vibrated with another call, but she ignored it.

* * *

Kevin finished the first draft of the brief for a mock trial and headed to the parking lot with phone in hand. "Di, I'm not giving up on us. If I have to, I'll fly, or I can drive Buffy Bug out. Let me know if you got this message." He tossed books and his backpack onto the passenger seat, started the car up, tore out of the parking lot, only to screech to a stop when a couple about to step off the curb jumped back in surprise. "Sorry," he mouthed. His palms were sweaty and his heart pounded.

The scraggly-haired man gave Kevin the single-fingered salute, repeated by his companion, a long-haired blonde of indeterminate gender. They ran toward the campus doubled over in laughter.

Kevin gripped the steering wheel and pulled into traffic. The run-in with the couple gave him the resolve he'd been lacking.

I'm not going to let those idiots ruin my day. I'll finish the semester and then head to Portland, if she's still there. I'll drive her car and we can come back together, or, no she can't refuse me, not after all we've been through.

Kevin pulled to the side of the street and punched in Diana's number. His call went immediately to voicemail, again.

* * *

In the privacy of their room and with Cassie fast asleep, Diana listened to Kevin's most recent message three times. *It sounds like he's coming.* She lay awake and ran multiple scenarios over in her mind: call him tomorrow and tell him she needed space; let him come; go to Naperville now for a face-to-face; or ask him to hold on until her tentative return in a few months. She couldn't sleep; her mind wouldn't shut off. *First thing in the morning I'll ask Cass. She always knows what to say. Even if it's not easy to hear.*

As if in response to Diana's thoughts, Cassie rolled over in her twin bed and asked, "Can't sleep?"

"Did I wake you up?"

"No, well, I *was* asleep, but I've been rustling around for a while. I had a feeling you were awake. Anyway, you weren't snoring." She chuckled.

"Thanks a lot. I can't sleep. I've been thinking about Kevin. He's left several messages, and I haven't had the guts to get back to him." She switched on the bedside lamp. Diana liked the soft light coming from the blue lampshade: twilight colors, her favorite time of the day.

Cassie propped herself on her elbow. "Trouble in paradise?"

Diana rubbed her twitchy left eye. "Kind of." She sat up, plumped her pillows, and leaned into them. "I think our summer romance happened way too fast, and then I went back to Boise for my senior year, and he was at Kent State so we only called and texted; and then he had his terrible accident." She waited a beat or two. "Maybe I should tell him we need more time, maybe tell him I need some space, maybe I should suggest he date other girls, maybe …"

"Whoa, how do you feel about him here?" Cassie pointed to her chest. "Do you love him?"

"I'm not sure." She looked down at her hands and tugged on a hangnail. "So if I'm not *sure*, then I must not be, and it wouldn't be fair to lead him on and get engaged because I feel sorry for him." She flopped onto her side and punched the pillow. "Wish I had Socks here to cuddle."

"A kitten will not solve your problems." Cassie hopped out of bed. "I can't handle serious topics tonight. What do you think about eating junk food and watching TV?"

"Great idea." Diana got up and put on her quilted robe. "Bundle up; they lower the heat at night."

The girls slipped out of their room and headed toward the stairs. "Watch for the third and fifth step, they squeak," Diana whispered. In the kitchen, she took bowls and glasses from the cupboard. "Cass, grab the popcorn and cookies from the pantry, and I'll check the fridge." Diana opened the door. "Do you want soda, orange juice, or milk?"

"Orange juice, please. And how about an apple? That way I can eat ice cream. The healthy stuff will cancel out the sugar." Cassie carried her armload to the counter and set it down.

"You haven't changed a bit, but cooking school might alter your eating habits."

"I saw a jar of trail mix in the cupboard. Nuts are good for you, aren't they?"

"Think so. I'll get the trays, drinks, and heat up the popcorn. Why don't you look in the cabinet next to the TV for a couple movies? Nothing too scary, though."

They settled down on either end of the sectional couch with blankets wrapped around their legs. While they watched most of season one of *The Big Bang Theory*, they devoured and refilled snacks. With full stomachs, they fell asleep by early morning.

James found the sleeping girls the next morning. He leaned over to kiss his daughter, but drew in a sharp breath when he saw she had been crying in her sleep.

CHAPTER 14
Best Laid Plans

ROBERTA SAT IN HER LAWYER'S reception area and fought off cravings for a smoke. She waited long enough to crave three cigarettes. "Damn."

The receptionist looked up. "May I get you something? A cup of coffee, perhaps?"

"Black, no sugar."

Sandra returned and placed a steaming mug on the coffee table, smiled, and sat behind her desk. Roberta took a sip and stared out the window. During her last appointment, she had imagined living amongst rich furnishings, thick carpets, enjoying the smell of mahogany and fresh flowers, owning original artwork and having a killer view of the city and surrounding hills. *Maybe I can snag Charles for good this go-round. We had a pretty hot past.* She smiled at the memories.

A few minutes later Charles entered the lobby and waved. "Hello, Roberta, shall we?"

"'Bout time." Roberta stood, walked the cup to Sandra's desk, and pushed it toward her; the remainder sloshed over the rim. "This coffee tastes like it's been sitting around all day." Sandra looked surprised, but dabbed the coffee stain off her paperwork, and appeared composed. Roberta greeted Charles with a crooked smile.

He led Roberta down the hall, opened the last door, and held it for her to go through. "Please, take a seat."

Roberta sat in the camel-colored leather chair opposite his desk and crossed her long legs. She hiked her skirt up a few inches and smiled.

"Was your little scene necessary?"

"Oh, chill, Charles."

"You're acting out again, like you're running scared. Cut the drama. Sandra doesn't need it, hell, I don't either." Charles sat at his desk and leaned back. "So, what do you have for me?"

Roberta hoped Charles had more in mind than a business meeting. She tilted her head flirtatiously. "Well ..." He frowned. "Sorry, I couldn't resist." She sat back and unbuttoned her jacket. "Okay, I have nothing concrete to give you, no paperwork; except I may be facing a lawsuit, or worse."

"Worse?"

"I don't know the technical terms. Let's call it *deep shit*."

Charles folded his hands across his chest and looked pensive for a moment. Without a word, he leaned forward and gave Roberta a look that sent chills down her spine. "We need to prepare for the worst. Child abduction across state lines has no statute of limitations for prosecution. This has likely gone up the chain. It is a federal crime, you know."

"No, I didn't know." Roberta slumped in her chair and kicked the front of the desk, then rummaged through her purse for a cigarette. "Aha." She tried to keep her hands steady as she lit it with an ornate silver lighter. She looked at Charles through her heavily-mascaraed eyelashes. "Remember, you gave this lighter to me. Was it Valentine's Day five years ago?"

Charles nodded. "And yes, I'll make an exception. You may smoke. Thanks for asking." He stood, walked to one of his bookcases, and pulled out a heavy volume. He flipped through a few pages. "This is serious, very serious. The police could show up at your door any minute." He approached Roberta. "Where are you staying?"

"With a friend."

"The same friend's house where the process-server allegedly tried to deliver papers ...when was that?"

"Yes, it happened a couple of weeks ago, at the most." She removed Charles' business cards from a crystal dish and flicked ashes into it. He frowned. "What? Is that dish an heirloom or something?"

"Expect him again. This will not go away. No matter how much you wish it were otherwise."

"Do I just wait for the hammer to fall?"

"We went through this a few months ago. And what did you do? You skipped town. Enough already, Roberta." He set the volume on his desk and came around the desk to face her. "Do you expect me to take your case pro-bono again?"

Roberta inhaled on her cigarette, tilted her head up, and held her breath a few seconds before she blew it toward Charles. "I have no money, no house, nada."

"So, nothing's changed." Charles crossed his arms and leaned against the desk. "I won't take you on unless you promise to act responsibly."

"Meaning what?"

"Meaning you stay in touch, stay in town, and *don't* lie to me."

Roberta was at a loss for words. Her stomach flip-flopped; she took one more drag on her cigarette, leaned forward, and crushed it in the dish. She exhaled. "Fine. Are we done?"

"For now. Is your cell number current with our records?" She nodded. Charles walked to the door and opened it. Roberta scurried past Sandra without a word.

* * *

Glenn called Kevin the day after his meeting with Big Stan. "Can we meet for lunch or dinner tomorrow?"

"Yes, sir, dinner would work."

"Fine. How are things going? Okay, I hope."

"Not bad, staying afloat in my classes, working on the weekends."

"Good. Big Stan and I had our meeting. I'd like to go over a few things we covered and talk about where we go from here."

"Where are we headed, exactly?"

"Hopefully we'll determine the thugs' identities. Also, we will consider why you were assaulted and kidnapped. I'm beginning to think it's a case of mistaken identity. It's possible this is linked to a campus drug ring or something broader. When pieces fall into place, I will request a grand jury to convene to determine if charges and a trial are justified."

"This could turn into a big deal," Kevin said.

"Correct. Are you up to it? If it moves forward, the process will take some time."

"I dunno. Right now so much is happening, uh, where should we meet?" Kevin asked.

"How about Red Robin, say seven o'clock? Remember that's where Diana introduced us."

"Seems like a million years ago." Kevin sighed.

"A lot has happened since then. I'll see you at seven," Glenn said.

CHAPTER 15
Onward and Upward

DIANA LEFT A MESSAGE ON KEVIN'S PHONE. "We *do* have to talk. It'd be better face-to-face, but we'll have to wait until after Thanksgiving. I'm spending it here with my parents and grandparents. Please call me."

Diana threw the phone on the bed and yanked on her braid; she unknotted her long hair and shook it out. She looked into the full-length mirror and giggled at her messy appearance, and how it reminded her of running at the beach with her sisters and feeling carefree. *Why does life have to get so complicated?* She flipped her hair back, tucked her blouse into her jeans, stared out the window, and wished for a clear answer.

The bedroom door flew opened. Cassie rushed in. "Hey, girlfriend, we're headed to the mall. Wanna come?" She fell onto Diana's bed and brushed back a stubborn curl that fell over her eyes. "What happened to your hair?"

Diana ran her fingers through a tangled mass of curls and shook it out. "I was exercising and it came loose. Anyway, who's going?"

"All of us girls, except your mother. I haven't been to Washington Square Mall. Is it pretty neat?"

"It's okay, but nothing like Chicago malls. When are you leaving?"

"Soon, so finish up with whatever." She glanced over to the phone. "Did you talk to Kevin?"

"I left him a message. I'll talk to him later, but not when we're out shopping."

"Uh, huh. Are you avoiding him?" Cassie twirled her hair and stuck a strand behind her ear.

"Not avoiding exactly, but I'm still not sure what to say."

"Be honest, don't lead him on, but don't be too hard either." Cassie stood and put her hands on her hips. "Remember how you felt when Roberta dropped the news about who your father might or might not be and then ignored you? She left you hanging."

"Yes." Diana lowered her head.

"Don't do the same thing with someone you care about. Even if it's not what he wants to hear, talk to him, tell him *something*. You are a nice person, not mean, like Roberta." The tone of her voice softened and she smiled. "So, still want to come with us?" Diana nodded. "Okay, see you in ten. I'm going to get a quick snack."

Cassie bounded out the door like a Labrador puppy. Diana smiled at her friend's enthusiasm.

Her phone chimed and she felt relieved to see Glenn's ID come up. "Hi, Dad. What's up?"

"I have an important update, but first, how about you, kiddo? Doing okay?"

"Yep, good. Cassie came out for an interview with the Oregon Culinary Institute and was accepted. She's enrolled and will be moving here after Christmas."

"Great, I'm glad to hear it. Big Stan is taking on Kevin's case, and you know how quickly he gets results. This could be a tough time for Kevin so I hope you'll be supportive."

Diana felt a stab of guilt. "Oh, sure. I, uh, hope he's feeling better and classes are going okay for him."

"Haven't you two talked recently?"

Diana fidgeted with the tassels on the bedspread. "We've been playing phone-tag. I'm getting ready to head out, so …"

"I'll cut this short. Take care, kiddo, and don't forget the phone works both ways."

"I'll try and call more often. Oh, give Socks a kiss from me." She heard Glenn chuckle before she hung up. Diana missed talking and cuddling with her kitten who gave no advice, no criticism, but offered feathery whisker-kisses and soft meows in return.

* * *

Roberta phoned Irma. "I won't be back for a while, maybe never. Can you pack my stuff into boxes and ship them to me?"

"Sorry to hear that, but I can't afford to ship your things. Let's see … how about sending me some money and I'll put them on a Greyhound bus?"

"A bus? Huh, let me think about it." Roberta paused. "Guess, I should let Sadie know I'm quitting the Rainbow. Or you could."

"I'd better not. She'd rather hear from you, Roberta."

"Okay. I'll text. How about I get you some money and you send me fifty-bucks' worth of belongings? Then I'll come back later and get the rest."

"How will I know what you need?"

"Pretend it's your stuff and take it from there." Roberta was getting annoyed and couldn't wait to end the call. "I have to go. I'll send you a money order in a couple days."

Zoë listened from the kitchen door. "I couldn't help overhearing the last part of your conversation. Are you planning to stay in Boise?" She hastened to add, "Naturally I'm happy at the prospect."

Roberta sat on the barstool and tossed her cell phone on the counter. "It seems like I'll have to. Things may be heating up."

"I'm so sorry." Zoë sat on the other barstool, pulled out her string of colored-glass beads from her skirt pocket, and fingered them like a rosary. "Maybe it's time to pull out the stops."

"What do you mean?"

Zoë spoke in hushed tones, "Did you know my family is from Cornwall, England?" Roberta shook her head. "Well, we have a tradition, no, not a tradition, but a deeply-held belief that wishes come true and illnesses and troubles can be cast away with a *cloutie.*"

Roberta grimaced and pulled a cigarette from her jeans' pocket. "A what?"

"A cloutie. It's a bit of fabric worn or held for a short time and then placed on the branch of a tree or bush in a sacred place, ideally at the Madron Well. But no matter where you are, with the right words said, a spell is cast and as the fabric disintegrates so do the owner's illness or trouble." Zoë sat back and smiled.

Roberta laughed so hard she started coughing. After regaining composure, she said, "I think you've completely lost your mind." She threw her unlit cigarette on the counter, got up, and poured a cup of coffee from the pot on the stovetop. She leaned against the counter. "I haven't heard anything so ridiculous in … like twenty years."

"Not so fast, my friend. You've been perfectly willing to have tarot card readings; we've spent hours around my crystal ball; I've read your palm; you trust in the zodiac signs, and follow your horoscope. Why not use a cloutie?"

Roberta sipped her coffee and stalled with her comeback. "Why the hell not? I guess there's no difference." She tossed the remainder of her coffee into the sink and stared out the window. "Zoë, I haven't been above board with you. I've been avoiding the truth." She leaned over the sink as though she'd be sick. "It's time to come clean. But I don't know where to start."

Her friend came over and put her hands on Roberta's shoulders. "Take your time. Come, sit. I'll make us some herbal tea."

Roberta sat at the kitchen table and started talking while Zoë put the kettle on the burner and measured out tea leaves.

* * *

Diana was sure something big was about to happen and the idea of talking to Kevin made her nervous. As she had expected, their conversation hadn't gone well. "I get the feeling you've been avoiding me. Diana. Are we okay?" Kevin asked.

"Kev, I was hoping you could come out for Thanksgiving. Then we can talk things out." She waited a beat or two. "And you could meet my family, too."

"Talk things out? Meet your family?" Diana heard him catch his breath. "I thought you were coming home after a few weeks."

"Plans have changed. I want to find out more about my birthplace and I need time to get to know my family. Dad's been on my case about college and for once, I agree with him. I'm looking into starting winter term here. If our love can last another year or two, then we're meant to be." She held her breath and waited, and waited.

"I see."

"Kev, remember our first Thanksgiving together? We weren't super serious *then*, and we had fun."

"Diana, you're talking ancient history."

"Please think about it. Cassie might still be here. She's been accepted to the Oregon Culinary Institute and starts in January. We're looking for an apartment to share. She'd love to see you."

She heard Kevin sigh. "If you say so. Tell Cassie I'd love to see her, too. I've always liked her. She's straight up." He paused. "I'll let you know by Halloween. Seems appropriate to let you know on the night goblins and witches are out." He chuckled and hung up.

CHAPTER 16
Peasants and Poets

"I'M FED UP WITH DAD calling so often. My life is my life and this *Kevin* investigation he's hanging over my head isn't going anywhere. I'm careful about who I sell stuff to and who I don't." Calvin pointed to Ted, his roommate. "You're a good example. Besides, he's beginning to sound like a drunk."

Ted was slumped on his bed puffing on a joint and blowing clouds of smoke toward the open window. "He's busy, uptight. Don't sweat it. He'll cover you. Even though he's not a hotshot New York lawyer, he's big enough to take on the bums you've been dealing drugs with."

Calvin stood and walked to the closet for a clean shirt. "Yeah sure, but his law partner isn't stupid and he's representing Kevin. You know, the guy who was mistaken for me and almost got beat to death last spring."

Ted inhaled and held his breath for a few seconds. He exhaled and squinted through the haze. "Love this stuff. Can you get more?"

"Find someone else. I'm backing off until things cool down."

"You gotta learn to chill, dude. Don't get uptight your senior year. Law school's coming up fast." Ted stood and threw his spent butt out the window where it landed in the bushes three floors below.

Calvin looked over his shoulder. "Be careful. We don't want the landlady finding them." He chuckled. "Hell, she may even ask for a stash of her own." He finished buttoning his shirt. "For now, I'll bet those goons won't let up. Someone followed me last night when I left the bar, so I had to drive five miles out of my way to lose them. Next time I may not be so lucky."

Ted snatched a beer from the fridge, popped the tab, and tore open a bag of chips. He sank into the worn leather recliner. "What did they want?"

Calvin adjusted his collar. "A pay-off. I owe two grand to the head honcho."

Ted pointed a taco chip in Calvin's direction. "From what you've said, they can't be too bright. They grabbed the wrong guy and wasted a lot of time and money. The boss must have been majorly pissed."

"The goon squad doesn't have to be smart, they just take orders. Hell, from what Dad said, they almost killed Kevin and dumped him in Canada when he couldn't cough up the money. And it could have been *me*." He put on a baseball cap. "I don't plan on coming back tonight, got lots of studying to do, so if you want female companionship, I won't interrupt." He smiled as he grabbed his coat, book bag, and phone. "Can I borrow your car? Just in case they're out there."

Ted nodded and pulled his keys from his pocket. He tossed them across the room. "Don't scratch it. It's only been out of the showroom a couple of weeks."

* * *

Irma received a fifty-dollar money order from Roberta and packed up two boxes for shipment. One of the clerks recognized her at the bus station. "Hey, wha'cha doing? Going on a trip?"

After she filled out the paperwork, Irma walked to her friend's ticket counter. "Hello, Kat. I'm shipping a couple of boxes to a friend." She rolled her eyes. "Not a friend exactly, more like a house guest who overstayed her welcome. I won't miss her cigarette smoke and sarcasm."

Kat seemed surprised. "I don't think I've ever heard you speak ill of someone. She must have been a real bitch."

Irma winced at 'bitch.' "I *do* try to give people the benefit of the doubt. But Roberta could push a saint to the Dark Side. I doubt she'll be back. As soon as she sends more money, I'll ship the rest of her stuff. What she doesn't need or want goes to charity."

Kat leaned forward. "Was she the gal who worked at the Rainbow? Long black braid, kind of snotty, uppity-like?"

"Yes, and I helped her get that job. But all she did was gripe about Sadie, the tips, and customers. It got old real fast."

"A couple of servers have worked there for like, twenty-five years. The Rainbow's a Pendleton landmark."

Irma pursed her lips. "It wasn't the management or customers. It was her." She lowered her voice. "I think Roberta was in trouble, deep trouble. Maybe with the law."

Kat's eyebrows arched. "Really?"

"I overheard a few phone calls and it didn't sound good. I think she was estranged from her daughter, too." Irma held up a forefinger. "But, I met one of her friends who came to visit from Boise not long ago. I think she delivered bad news; then Roberta left. Anyway, her friend seemed very nice, warm, genuine, though a little different."

"How so?"

"Oh, she's into palm reading, wore beads, dangly earrings." She fluttered her hand under her ear. "And a long, full, patchwork skirt." With a shrug, she said, "And for some reason she liked Roberta. I think Roberta rented a room from Zoë."

Kat smiled. "Cool name. Sounds exotic. Say, let's meet up for coffee. We haven't talked in ages."

"Good idea. I'll give you a call." Irma waved goodbye.

* * *

Diana and Cassie lounged on the twin beds unsure of how to spend their Saturday. "Cass, I've been thinking of cutting my hair off."

"You're kidding. How short?"

Diana held her hand just below her ear. "I want an A-line bob. Something easy. I'm tired of dealing with so much hair, and now Kevin isn't around telling me what to do, I can style it however I want."

"Did he really tell you how to wear your hair?" Cassie sat up in apparent surprise.

Diana stroked her hair and rotated her shoulder. "He made it clear he preferred girls with long hair. He said it was *sexier*."

Cassie tugged at her short curls. "Every time I try to grow mine out, it looks goofy. My hair isn't thick enough; it has a mind of its own."

"You look perfect. Don't change for anyone." Diana stood, walked to the window, and aimed her conversation at the red maple tree. "I invited Kevin for Thanksgiving, but I'm not sure he'll come. He said he'd let me know by Halloween, then laughed and hung up."

"Really?" Cassie's voice seemed to brighten. "Super."

"He said he'd love to see you. Maybe you can give him a call and encourage him to come."

"You'd be okay with me calling Kevin?"

"Sure! All's fair ... besides, he said, 'Cassie's straight up,' whatever that means." She shrugged. "I think he thinks I'm getting ready to break up with him."

"Aren't you?"

"Not exactly, but I'm not ready to commit long term."

Cassie leaned back and kicked off her slippers. One landed on Diana's bed. "Then don't play games."

"Huh?"

"It sounds like you're tired of him." Cassie pulled on her silver, looped earring. "I've had a huge crush on him ever since you guys stayed with us in Boise. Mom would have said something if she hadn't been so sick from chemo."

Diana sat on the bed. "I don't know why I didn't notice before. You're my best friend, my oldest friend. I'd never try to use you."

"Not intentionally. But, I could be the solution to your little problem. Kevin's confused, vulnerable, and could fall for the first girl who smiles at him. I don't want to hurt him now, or ever."

"I feel sick." Diana held her stomach and leaned over. When she looked up, she had tears in her eyes. "You're disappointed in how I'm treating Kevin. Kevin's ticked off with me." She wiped her wet cheek. "I'm a terrible person."

Cassie moved next to Diana and rubbed her friend's back in circular motions. "No, you're stressed, mixed up, and maybe a little scared. You've been through a lot. Most people would be doing drugs by now, gone wacko, or both. Your mother ... I mean Roberta, stole the first eighteen years of your life and practically ruined your parents' lives. But you've come through stronger than most." She stopped to wipe her nose with the back of her hand. Diana looked at her with tear-filled eyes. Cassie continued, "I love you, your folks love you, Glenn loves you, Kevin loves you. Who could love a 'terrible' person?"

Diana hugged her friend and whispered, "I don't deserve you." She pulled back and wiped her wet cheeks. "So, you have a crush on Kevin?"

Cassie smiled. "Guilty." She bounced up. "I have an idea. Let's go to the animal shelter." She held up two fingers. "And pick out two kittens. One for me, one for you. Maybe they'll be friends by the time we move into our apartment."

Diana hiccupped. "You're changing the subject."

"So what? I dropped a bombshell and now we need something fun to think about. Wash your face and let's find two of the cutest fur bundles in Portland."

"My brother's allergic."

"All the more reason to find our own place ASAP. In the meantime, they can stay in our room."

"I think Mom would be okay with that." She jumped up. "I'm not sure where the County Animal Shelter is, but we could go to one of the pet stores. Then we could buy food, a kitty bed, and toys."

Cassie checked her purse. "I have some cash left. You saved me wads of money by letting me stay here instead of a hotel."

"What are friends for? I'll ask Mom if I can borrow the car. Be right back."

CHAPTER 17
Legal and Spiritual Concerns

GLENN ANSWERED A CALL FROM BIG STAN. "Sir, I've been thinking on your offer and decided to accept. I'm not getting any younger, and we get along well. This could give me the financial security I need heading to retirement."

Glenn leaned back in his leather chair. "Retirement? That's years away. With my connections and your modern-day *Sherlock Holmes* approach, we'll have the best team in the mid-west. But we still have to talk salary."

"Not worried in the least. You've been more than fair, generous. Just let me know when I can move my things over. Won't bring much, just a computer and a file cabinet. I do have some artwork and a small stereo. They help me relax, think straight."

Glenn felt a sense of relief. "You'll have plenty of room. The office is ready for you on the third floor, just below mine. There's a desk, bookcase, and you can use my secretary if need be. This should be an easy transition."

"Uncomplicated, sir, just as I like it."

"Anything new to report on Kevin's case?"

"Not over the phone. I can say things are moving along. But, I'll need to head out of town again."

"Understood, so when can I expect you to arrive?" Glenn asked.

"If it's okay, Monday, first thing."

"Fine. See you then." Glenn was going to say goodbye, but Big Stan ended the call. He chuckled at Stan's no-nonsense manner as he rose and poured a cup of coffee from the thermos on the credenza. Glenn stirred in a generous helping of cream. *Celebration time. Screw the calories.* He looked out the window and enjoyed the view for the first time in weeks.

* * *

Roberta sat in her attic apartment at Zoë's home and considered her options. She could wait on the next move by the Williamses; ignore all bad news from her lawyer; contact Diana; call Glenn and give him another sob story; skip town again. She shook her head. *No, that's a terrible idea. But maybe I can talk Diana out of this insanity, let bygones be bygones. If it weren't for Zoë, I don't know where I'd be now. A friend in need.*

She heard a soft tap and a voice at her door asking, "May I come in?"

"Enter, my friend."

Zoë entered the room holding a wooden tray with two mugs of steaming tea and a plate of cookies. Roberta smiled. "Irma liked to end the day with herbal tea and homemade cookies. It didn't make a crappy day better, but was a nice gesture. As silly as she was, the woman had a good heart. Come, sit." She patted the edge of her bed.

Zoë moved the lamp aside and set the tray on the bedside table. She sat on the end of the bed, spread out her skirt, and folded her hands. "Roberta, I've been thinking ever since you told me the truth about you and Diana; how about taking a new approach? Why don't you call Diana? Better yet, talk to her parents. Maybe they don't want this legal mess any more than you do. Settle with them."

Roberta leaned over, grabbed a cookie, and took a bite. After swallowing, she said, "Settle? How? I doubt they'll be in the mood to *settle* for a 'Sorry for stealing your baby girl.' They might be forgiving types, but not pushovers."

"Even so, make the first move. I've been thinking long and hard about this. My tarot cards tell me it's possible to end this matter without confrontation. Maybe if you soften your heart a bit, ask for forgiveness. You won't regret it, Roberta."

"*Forgiveness*. You've got to be kidding. They'll pounce and then go for the kill. I won't give them the chance. No way."

"This is serious. You could end up in jail. People don't like to be taken advantage of, tricked, and lied to. From what you've shared, they've had plenty of that."

Roberta finished her tea before she answered, "Lots to think about. But I doubt my lawyer would agree with you. He won't let me give in." She made a fist. "He's a fighter."

"I forgot about him. He would know all the legal angles. But, we have the supernatural at our disposal: tarot cards, crystal ball, Ouija board, the cloutie. You haven't forgotten, have you?"

"Right. I hang a rag on your dogwood tree and in a few weeks all my problems disappear." She poured another cup of tea and put two cookies on a napkin.

"Not quite so simple. You have to have *faith*, Roberta. Faith and total commitment to solving your problems."

"Sure."

"One more thing. I have a student who is almost ready to take on her own clients. She'll be at my gathering tonight for her last lesson. May I have her sit in on your next reading?"

"Sure, why not?" Roberta leaned against the headboard and stuffed a pillow under her knees. "Plan on baking anything else?"

"I am, actually. The ladies love my cookies as much as you." Zoë stood. "Why don't you help me in the kitchen and then we'll hang the cloutie."

Roberta was surprised. "Give me a few minutes. I have to make a phone call."

A couple of hours later, the women stood beneath the dogwood tree in Zoë's backyard. "I picked out a special piece of cloth for you." Zoë withdrew a scarlet hanky embossed with white hearts from her skirt pocket. "This belonged to my late sister. We were very close."

"I didn't know you had a sister."

"Aurora was my identical twin and soul-sister in every way. She passed away from cancer ten years ago."

Roberta hesitated to accept the gift. "But why would you want to hang it out in the weather knowing it will be ruined?"

"Aurora was truly gifted and you need the strongest charm possible." Zoë choked back a sob. "She had a kind and generous heart and I have no doubt she would approve."

Roberta was touched. "This is the nicest thing anyone has done for me. Thank you."

Zoë smiled. "Here you go, then. Hold it close to your heart while you think of a few words you want to say. Then, hang it as high as you can reach, utter your wishes out loud, and let nature and the spirits take over."

Roberta accepted the cloth, touched it to her cheek, and inhaled. "It's infused with lavender."

Zoë nodded. "It was her signature fragrance. Every time I smell lavender, I think of Aurora."

Roberta held the hanky to her breast and murmured a few words. Zoë said, "You must say it out loud so the spirits will hear you."

* * *

Diana found her mother in the kitchen holding a wooden spoon and peering at a cookbook. "Mom, you could win the *Good Housekeeping* award. You practically live in here." Emily turned and Diana smiled at the specks of flour freckling her mother's nose.

"True, true, but I love it. It takes me back to the times spent in the kitchen with Gran and Mama. They taught me all they knew: improvising recipes when they didn't have all the ingredients, cooking for huge crowds at holidays, even cake decorating. For a while I ran my own business and made custom cakes for weddings and special occasions."

"Cool."

Emily took off her glasses and rubbed her nose. "Tickles. Gosh, I'm covered with flour."

"I was about to say something." Diana handed her a towel.

"Thanks. Anyway, since I was able to stay home with the kids, this became my office. But you didn't come in to listen to ancient history. I have the feeling you want to tell me something."

Diana sat on the barstool, took a deep breath, and rubbed her twitchy left eye before she dropped the news. "Cassie and I have decided to find an apartment to share, and we'd like to adopt two kittens, but we'll keep them upstairs for now since Bryan is allergic."

"My goodness." Emily sat on the adjoining barstool and leaned in close. "Perhaps I shouldn't ask this, but how will you pay the rent and such?"

"Dad, I mean Glenn, started a college fund for me *years* ago, and I have savings. So I should be okay."

After a full half-minute, Emily said, "I'm surprised, but not shocked. Your father and I knew one day you'd be moving out. But we were reunited only a few months ago."

"Mom, I …"

Emily held up her hand. "No need to explain. I suspect growing up with that neglectful woman, you had to make many decisions on your own. You must have felt so lonely." Emily blinked quickly and gazed out the window.

Diana reached for her mother's hand and gave it a squeeze. "Glenn and I were close. I thought he was my real dad for seventeen years." Emily nodded. "After he and Roberta divorced he moved away, but we talked on the phone every week. And I saw him summers and holidays. Plus, I had Cassie's mother to talk to. She's been awesome."

"Diana, we love you and wish you nothing but happiness. If getting an apartment with Cassie is what you want, we won't be difficult."

Bryan burst into the room and headed straight for the refrigerator. He stuck his head in and kept it there long enough for Emily to say, "Bry, choose your snack and close the door, please."

"Don't rush me." He pulled his head out and gave her his lopsided grin.

Emily pointed to the cookie jar. "Oatmeal raisin, your favorite. Get a plate and whatever you want to drink, take it to the den or family room. Your sister and I are talking."

"Huh, girlie stuff." Bryan grabbed a Coke and four cookies. "Don't want to overhear something I shouldn't." He made a sour-lemon expression.

"We'll be done shortly, hon."

"'K, fine." Bryan left as abruptly as he had come.

Emily made sure he was out of earshot. "One thing, let's talk to your father right away. Your sisters will be disappointed. Bryan will miss you too, I'm sure." She smiled and patted Diana's hand. "You're a wonder. Being raised by such a hateful woman and you are so perfect."

Diana laughed. "Hardly." She paused. "But I would like to legally change my name to Diana Julia Louise Williams. Then, everything *will* be perfect."

Emily caught her breath and her eyes filled with tears and they spilled down her cheeks. "My darling girl." She leaned over and pulled Diana close. They held each other until Bryan came back for more cookies.

"What'd I miss?"

CHAPTER 18
Win One, Lose One

"CALVIN WHERE THE HECK ARE YOU? And what's up with my car?" Ted had left several messages and checked with Calvin's friends when he didn't call or return by 4 p.m. the next day. No one knew of his whereabouts. On day two, Ted filed a stolen vehicle report and on the third day, he called Calvin's father.

"No, I haven't heard from my son. And what in the hell were you thinking by waiting so long to report him missing? Did he tell you where he was headed?"

"He was going to study for mid-terms, so maybe the library. But he also said he wouldn't be back that night, so he might have met one of his girlfriends and stayed over. I checked with a couple, no luck. I'm kind of pissed. The last thing I told him was to not scratch my new car." Ted took a long drag on his joint, choked, and couldn't finish his thought.

"Damn it. How can you worry about a stupid car at a time like this? Calvin is missing. You've wasted precious time." John sounded furious.

Ted crushed his spent joint in an overflowing ashtray. "Hey, I did the best I could. He's probably hanging with one of his friends, lost track of time. You know how it is."

"*No*, I don't know. By everything holy, you'll have plenty to answer for if something's happened to him. I'll be on the first flight to Cleveland."

* * *

John hung up, stormed out of his office, headed toward the lobby, and barked at his assistant. "Cancel all of my appointments for the entire week, maybe the next."

"What about today's deposition and your court schedule?"

"I said cancel *everything*. Calvin has been missing for three days." Susan gasped, dropped her pen, and stood in obvious shock. "The only messages or calls I want forwarded to my cell are from the police or my private investigators, and naturally Calvin. I'm heading to Kent State to find my son."

He slammed the exterior office door on his way out; a second later, he heard what sounded like breaking glass and guessed the vibration had sent his prized Oriental vase crashing to the floor.

* * *

A deputy ushered John into Police Chief Brady's office and made introductions. Before the chief could utter a word, John poked his finger at him. "My son, Calvin Bergan, borrowed his roommate's Corvette on Friday. This is Tuesday and no one has seen or heard from him. I get to town and find someone reported a red Corvette ended up at the bottom of a ravine - with a burned body inside."

Brady cleared his throat. "Correct. Early this morning a hiker found a crashed vehicle about thirty miles out of town. First responders confirmed the incident, but I can't go into more detail until the next-of-kin is notified."

"Where does the case stand?" John loosened his collar and tried to collect his thoughts. All he could think of was finding Calvin.

"The coroner has removed the body, the site has been taped off, and forensics are on the scene."

John stepped closer and handed Chief Brady his business card. "I'm a lawyer with plenty of experience, so don't hold anything back thinking I won't understand or can't handle the truth. And don't ever give me a line of bull. I can smell it a mile away." John ignored the chief's apparent attempt to inject a comment. "Finding my son is my first priority, so I have to be kept in the loop."

"Sir, it will be a while before we can ID the victim. It may not be your son. Be assured we'll notify you of the medical examiner's findings if it's Calvin."

"Chief, I can't wait until some flunky who couldn't make it as a real doctor has cut open my boy or checked his dental records. I have connections and expect you to make this your top priority." He removed a silver cigar cutter and a cigar from his coat pocket, snipped off the end, and flicked it in the waste basket.

"*No* smoking." Chief Brady crossed his burly arms over his chest.

John held the cigar in mid-air. "I'm ready to hitch a ride or get directions for a first-hand look." He put the cigar back in his pocket, walked to the window, and looked out. "This smells more like foul play and the deliberate planting of false evidence staged for the lazy or *dumb*."

"If you'd like to go with me, I'll be ready in ten, fifteen minutes. However, you won't be able to get too close."

"I'll be in the lobby. Have a few calls to make before we leave." John strode off.

* * *

John stood outside of the police cruiser at the edge of the highway and looked down at the tire ruts, broken bushes, and tree branches littering the hillside to the crash site. He held his hand above his eyes to shield the sun's glare and calculated how far to the bottom. *Three hundred feet straight down. Never had a chance.*

Clouds of dust swirled around John's legs as he headed down to see the team gathered around the twisted Corvette which was incongruous with its wooded surroundings. His heart raced as he waded through the heavy blanket of fall leaves. He swallowed and nearly choked as dry air filled his throat. At the bottom, John stood behind the yellow tape, but close enough to eavesdrop on two men in uniform.

"What do you think?" the younger asked the older officer.

"If I didn't know better, I'd say it was the work of Mafia-types or a lesser drug dealer. But I haven't seen this kind of activity in a couple of years." He took off his cap and scratched his head. "The chief called a few minutes ago. He's bringing a Mr. Bergan over. The victim could be his son." He leaned in closer. "The Chief warned me he acts like he has a chip on his shoulder and is *plenty* full of himself."

The young man nodded. "We can handle him." He rocked back on his heels. "Let me get this right; a hiker found a banged-up Corvette with a body inside, completely toasted, but the car hadn't caught on fire. Weird."

John had heard enough. He moved and when he stepped on a fallen branch, the officers turned around in apparent surprise. "I'm John Bergan and I don't have a chip on my shoulder, but I do expect you to pull out all the stops." He held up a forefinger. "Put pressure on the coroner to determine who the victim is ASAP." He raised another finger. "My son, Calvin, has been missing for four days. If the John Doe *isn't* my son, then put your best men out there and find him."

The older officer replaced his cap and held out his hand in greeting. John ignored the gesture. "We didn't mean to get off on the wrong foot. I'm Officer Reynolds. Be assured, we have our best working on this case."

John knotted his hands into fists and slowly released them. "How long have you men been on the force?"

"Ten years."

"Two." The young man held up his fingers, then lowered his hand and rested it on his belt.

"Who does the car belong to?" John pointed to the wreck.

"We can't tell you that until we know who the victim is, sir," the older cop said.

John suppressed a few curse words that popped into his mind. "I want to see the body, again, ASAP."

"But ..." the officer tried to intervene.

"Here's my card." John thrust his business card at the officer. "I'll be in town for as long as it takes to find my son. I'm sure we'll run into each other again." John wheeled around and headed back up the hill. He glanced back and saw the officers looking at each other and shrugging.

* * *

"I'm not asking for details, but you say John took off for Cleveland when he heard Calvin was missing?" Glenn asked Susan, his law partner's assistant, the next morning.

Susan nodded. "Yes, sir." She sniffled. "He said, 'I'm heading to Kent State to find my son.'"

"Anything else?"

"Not really. All I know is, he took a call, was on the phone for five, ten minutes, and then flew out the door. When he left, he slammed the door so hard his Oriental vase fell off its pedestal. I don't want the cleaning crew to get blamed."

"Okay. I'm going to find out what's going on." Glenn approached her desk and softened the tone of his voice. "You are aware John and I had a bit of a falling out over one of my clients."

She looked away and played with the computer mouse. "Yes."

"We might part ways professionally. It's been what, fifteen years we've been law partners?"

"I think so."

"This could affect you. I mean, you might have to move if John leaves the firm. But I'm sure you will keep your job."

She looked up. "I hope so. But right now I'm more worried about Calvin and Mr. Bergan, not about my job."

"Me, too. When I find out what's going on, I'll let you know. Why don't you forward the phones, lock up, and go for a walk or get a cup of coffee?" Glenn smiled. "Take your time."

"I will. Thanks."

He crossed the lobby to his secretary's desk, left her a note to not disturb him until after lunch, and went to his office. He locked the door, pulled the drapes, washed down his migraine medication with a glass of water, and stretched out on the couch. *God, my head hurts. Our feud has given me the first migraine I've had in ages.* Glenn laid as still as he could and stared at the ceiling for a half hour. Feeling frustrated, he took a few deep breaths, turned on his side, and tried to think pleasant thoughts. He finally dropped off to sleep an hour later.

* * *

"Who would have thought it'd be so hard to find an apartment in our price range?" Diana asked. "Maybe we should look south in Sherwood or Wilsonville. They're farther out and the rent might be less." She took a gulp of her Starbucks' Mocha Macchiato and tucked her feet up into the leather chair.

"But the bus ride would take twice as long and I'm not a morning person. Do you know anyone who'd like to share expenses?" Cassie asked.

"Nope. I don't know anyone in Portland except family. Rats, I was hoping we could move before Thanksgiving, by Christmas latest. I feel bad for the kittens being shut up in our bedroom. They're getting bored."

"How can they be bored? They have plenty of room and the cat toys you bought keep them busy."

"Anyway, Mom and Dad will be happy I won't be moving out anytime soon."

"I kinda feel sorry for your folks. I mean, they lost you as a baby, missed your whole childhood, found you eighteen years later, and now you're leaving."

"I'm staying in town. Just won't be seeing them every day. Nobody seems to get it. I *have* to be on my own. I feel smothered living with five other people."

Cassie nodded. "We both grew up as an only child. Except I was loved by my mom and Roberta was awful to you, to everyone really."

"No kidding. It's too bad Dad is feeling lonely since I moved out here. He sounds kind of down when we talk, and complains he and Socks watch too much TV. But, he and your mom are moving right along. I wonder when they'll take the plunge."

"Mom is finished with her cancer treatments, but wants a clean bill of health. I think the cancer has been holding her back from being engaged. Didn't think I'd say this, but I'm looking forward to her putting the house up for sale and moving to Naperville because ..."

"Then she and Dad will be married and we'll be *sisters*." Diana leaned forward and squeezed Cassie's hand. "I'm going to get a cookie, want one?"

"No thanks. I'm trying to cut down. As soon as classes begin, I'll be sampling everything. Don't want to blimp up beforehand."

"Silly, you've always been thin." Diana grabbed her purse. "I'll be right back." She stopped by the pastry counter before she got in line behind four others. When her phone rang, she answered before she saw Roberta's ID pop up.

"Diana."

"Yes, oh, it's you."

"Yes, missy, and it's about time we talked about this lawsuit crap."

"Roberta, I can't say anything. It's not up to me."

"Listen, I'm broke, so your *folks* might as well give it up. You won't see a dime."

"It's not about money."

"No? What else matters?"

"Justice."

"Isn't that sweet. Justice. According to the Bible, aren't you supposed to forgive your trespassers?"

"Don't twist things around. You always blame me for your problems. I never want to talk to you again." Diana hung up, shoved her phone in her purse, and stepped forward to order three giant chocolate chip cookies.

CHAPTER 19
Déjà Vu

THREE DAYS LATER Calvin's groggy brain overcame the drugs his captors had administered through an IV. *What the hell happened? Where am I?* A moment later, he wondered. *What day is this?* His orderly mind struggled to make sense of the situation. Through half-opened eyes, he concluded he was in a darkened room with a shadowy form sitting a few feet away. Calvin waited a minute or two and when it didn't move, he tried to sit up, but couldn't. *Good god, I'm paralyzed.*

He tried to raise his hand to touch his throbbing face, but his arm muscles wouldn't obey. Calvin stifled the urge to scream and frantically twisted his arms, legs, and ankles. When he discovered they were tightly bound, he took a deep breath, exhaled, and tilted his head up. The movement induced a pounding headache and sharp chest pains; his head fell with a *thump. I'm not paralyzed, I'm tied up.*

Loud voices from an adjoining room and what sounded like furniture being scraped across the floor came through the door. Calvin managed to move his aching head and saw a sliver of light beam across the floor. *Who are they? What do they want?* But he feared the answer to both questions.

Calvin's captors seemed occupied, so he had time to think. *I remember, I was headed for the car, grabbed from behind, and then thrown into a van.* He blinked several times to clear his head. *This is what Kevin must have gone through last spring; except Kevin didn't know why he was kidnapped. It was all a mistake.*

He struggled against the constraints, but couldn't loosen them. His eyes had adjusted well enough to see pinholes of light coming from a partially blacked-out window. When he realized the solitary shape across the room was a large chair and not a bodyguard, he made a quick calculation: *The window is at least eight feet up, but if I can get loose, I might be able to stand on the chair and climb out.*

The voices subsided, then a distant door slammed shut. At the sound of approaching footfalls, he panicked. *I'm not a praying man, but this would be the time to start. Maybe I can negotiate. I have enough cash stashed away to make a deal, but they'll want interest and not the monetary kind. I'll probably be beaten to a pulp.*

* * *

"Kevin, do you have a few minutes? I have some news to share."

"Sure, Mr. Baker. I was thinking about giving you a call."

"Enough of the *Mr.* bit. It's Glenn. Calvin has gone missing, four days now, and as soon as John heard, he hopped on the first flight to Cleveland."

"Wow. Normally I wouldn't care about Calvin one way or the other, but this could be serious. I know him. It's mid-term and he'd never miss exams his senior year. He's an ass, but plenty smart and will go clear to the top, maybe into politics." Kevin laughed. "He has the personality for it."

"To quote an old saying, 'The chickens have come home to roost.'"

"About time," Kevin said.

"I hadn't heard from John, so I checked online and saw on Monday hikers found a banged-up Corvette at the bottom of a ravine just outside Kent. The kicker is, a male was found at the wheel, charbroiled; the car looked like it had been through a giant wringer, not a fire."

"Man oh man, as much as I dislike Calvin, I sure hope it's wasn't him."

"I'll keep you posted. On the home front, Big Stan has moved into my building and is hard at work on your case and a half dozen more. Don't know how I got along before he came onboard fulltime."

"That's good to hear. I may be in Portland over Thanksgiving. Cassie's staying with Diana; she's going to cooking school in January. I'd like to see Cassie, find out what's new, and how her mother is feeling."

"Oh?"

"Yes. I've always thought Cassie was *real*, not caught up in herself."

Glenn needed a moment to absorb the last comment. "I'll miss you two. Guess I'll take Maggie to my sister's for Turkey Day dinner."

"Maggie, Cassie's mom? I forgot you're dating."

"Yes, we are." Glenn chuckled.

"Let me know how it goes with Calvin and his dad. Whatever happens, it will affect me and the investigation."

"You can depend on it, Kevin. Give Diana a hug and kiss from me."

"Sure."

"As Diana's father and your friend, I'm concerned about you. I hope you can iron out whatever problems you two may be having."

"It's not up to me, sir."

* * *

After ending the conversation with Diana, Roberta slammed her phone on the bed so hard it bounced onto the floor. "Damn that girl and her so-called family. I can't live like this. There has to be a way to stop their BS investigation from going forward."

She went to the window, leaned her forehead against the glass, and looked at the backyard. It was so peaceful and perfect, it could have been a garden out of a dream rather than Roberta's world. The cloutie stirred in the breeze, but held fast to the branch. For an instant, she thought about running again. But where?

She pounded her fist on the window sill and mentally dug in her heels. Her philosophy had been to not look back unless there was a score to settle and to never regret past decisions. In her mind, she didn't make mistakes, others did, and she was collateral damage.

Tears came unexpectedly. She wiped them away with the back of her hand, but when a childhood memory flooded back, it knocked her off balance. Roberta saw herself lying in bed in her own attic room, crying herself to sleep.

Ever since I was a little girl, people have used me. Mama made me pretend to be a psychic and cheat people. Then Daddy would beat me when I didn't bring in enough money to feed his drinking and gambling addictions. How many nights did I go to bed hungry?

Roberta retrieved her ringing phone from the floor and saw Charles' office number. She sniffled and gathered her composure. It rang three more times before she answered, "Hello."

"Mrs. Baker, this is Sandra, Mr. Carson's assistant. He would like you to make an appointment for this week if possible."

Roberta sighed in relief. "Great minds think alike. I have to see him. Soon."

"How about tomorrow at ten o'clock?"

"I'll be there." She hung up, glanced in the mirror, and winked. "Hello gorgeous. You're back." She hopped down two stairs at a time to the kitchen. *Good karma. I can feel it. I have my health, a bed to sleep in, and the will to beat this. Now I just need the way. Charles won't let me down. And, I have Zoë. She has the gift, the third eye, no hocus-pocus bullshit like Mama and I passed off to pathetic losers.*

Zoë was visiting one of her psychic friends, so Roberta raided her secret stash of brownies. She chuckled remembering how Zoë had made a big deal of staying away from sweets. *We all need a little sugar to get through tough times.*

* * *

Roberta entered Charles' office where, without a word, he gestured for her to sit. Roberta was puzzled by his silence. She perched on the edge of her chair and leaned forward. "What's going on?"

"It's like this: I've been trying to set up a phone conference with opposing counsel, John Bergan; however, I've been told he is 'not available until further notice.'"

"What the hell does that mean?"

Charles leaned back and crossed his arms over his chest. "I'm not sure, but I'm thinking an emergency came up."

"Now what? Do we wait for them to make the next move?"

Charles stood and came around to her side of the desk. "I have an idea how to respond in a way as to not waste my time drafting a brief; at least until I see the charges in black and white."

"Waste *your* time? What am I supposed to do in the meantime? Sit on my hands?"

"Berta, I'm sorry. Bergan is most likely working with the district attorney's office, so this *is* serious. I won't kid you. If you are found guilty, you could go to jail."

Roberta gasped, lowered her head, and said in a whisper, "My worst nightmare." Visions of being locked in her room as a child flashed in her mind. Her eyes welled over.

"I can't change things. It is what it is," Charles said.

She winced. "I hate that saying. Don't trivialize this. I can't be locked up. I'd go mad. I'll kill myself first."

Charles handed her a box of tissues. "Don't relive your suicide attempt. You may succeed next time." He crossed his arms and spoke in a soft voice, "I'd hate to see you do something stupid."

Roberta slumped in the chair and cried as hard as she had when she realized Diana was never coming home. She cried for her daddy when he beat her and told her he hated her. She cried for lost chances, poor decisions, and no going back.

Charles leaned down and put his arms on her shaking shoulders, and his kind gesture made her cry all the harder.

CHAPTER 20
Wishin' and Hopin'

"DIANA, YOU FOUND US AN APARTMENT!" Cassie jumped on the bed and sent the kittens skittering under the bed. "Oops, sorry, little ones. Hey, what are we going to name these critters?"

Diana smiled. "How about Wishin' and Hopin'?"

"How did you come up with those names?"

"They're from the title of one of the pop songs from the sixties I grew up on. Roberta was weird, but she had good taste in music. She listened to classical as well as the oldies."

Cassie rolled her eyes and looked at the ceiling. "Wishing and Hoping."

"*Wishin'* and *Hopin'*, no *g*. I feel like that these days, not in the romantic way like Dionne Warwick's song, but I'm wishin' and hopin' for everything to work out."

Cassie hung over the edge of the bed and called, "Hey, Wishin' come on out."

"Who are you calling?"

"*My* kitty. See his tiny white marking on his forehead? The rest of him is as black as the night sky. *When you wish upon a star,*" Cassie sang. When he popped from under the bed, she picked him up, kissed his face, and set him on her lap, where he squirmed a bit before settling in.

"It's the theme song from Disney's *Pinocchio*." Diana patted the floor. "Come here, Hopin'." Her kitty's nose, whiskers, and button eyes appeared from under the dust ruffle. "You look so much like Sockies. I can't wait until you meet," she crooned.

"Hey, if Kevin comes out next month, maybe he can bring Socks," Cassie said.

"I'll ask the next time we talk." She picked up Hopin' and nuzzled her soft grey and white fur. "Or I could text."

"What a chicken way out. *Talk* to him. You guys were practically engaged." She jumped when her kitten hopped off her lap and ran for the window. "Oww, Wishy, your nails are sharp." Cassie rubbed her leg. "I got sidetracked. What's our apartment like?"

Diana plopped down on her bed. "It's above a garage and fully furnished with two bedrooms, a big living room, fireplace, bath, laundry and kitchenette. Only six hundred a month, plus utilities."

"Over a garage?" Cassie wrinkled her nose.

"A five-car garage on an estate. Have you seen Audrey Hepburn in *Sabrina*?" Cassie shook her head. "It's an old movie, but you'd love it. We'll have to rent it sometime." Diana smiled. "If Audrey Hepburn can live above a garage, I guess we can, too."

Cassie fell back onto the bed and spread out her arms. "You're right. Who would ever have thought I'd be living on an estate."

"Just to let you know, the main house is sort of rundown and looks a little creepy on the outside. But the inside is beautiful, full of antiques, art, and books. Lots of books."

Cassie sat up. "Creepy?"

Diana scrunched her nose. "Creepy isn't the right word. More like mysterious, maybe even *romantic*. We drove down a long drive through acres of woods. I thought we were lost and then this grand old house appeared, like out of a gothic novel."

"Who's 'we' and how did you find it?"

"Mrs. Crenshaw, Mom's next door neighbor, took me this morning. You were still asleep and I didn't want to bother you." Cassie sighed. "Sorry. Anyway, her elderly cousin, Charlotte Winchester, lives there and is looking for a tenant for her apartment."

"Is she an old maid?"

"Yes, but Miss Winchester's nephew lived with her for a few years. When he graduated from high school, he moved to Amity to help with the family farm. There are a bunch of Winchesters living in the Willamette Valley. Back to Miss W – she has a couple of servants, a gardener, and chauffeur. The estate has *great* atmosphere and would be the perfect setting for a Halloween party and a scavenger hunt." Diana grinned. "Why don't we go tonight? It's only a few miles away. Once you see it, you'll love it."

"In the dark? I don't think so. How about tomorrow?"

"Let's go tonight. I'll call and make an appointment. Don't worry."

"Famous last words," Cassie said.

* * *

Diana and Cassie left for the Winchester estate that evening just before sunset. Cassie gripped the armrest and took long, deep breaths. "Are you sure this is the right road? You've been driving in circles for an hour. I've seen the same trees five times."

"Trees are trees. Wait, see the lights over there? That's it, I'm sure." Diana pointed and made a right turn.

"So, is Miss W like everyone's favorite aunt who bakes cookies and knits scarves?" Cassie picked at a loose string on her sweater and glanced out the window. "I could use a new sweater." She gave a nervous giggle.

"She's sweet. Mrs. Crenshaw told me the garage apartment has been vacant for a year, and she hinted Miss Winchester needs the income." Diana spotted the massive wrought iron gate with the elaborate *W* at the top. "Here we are. Get out and help me open the gate, please."

"This isn't a great way to start. It should have been left open for us."

Diana called over her shoulder as she exited the car, "This morning Mrs. Crenshaw and I had to open it and the footman asked us to close it when we left. They don't want just *anybody* driving in."

"No one in their right mind would be coming here," Cassie muttered.

Diana waited for Cassie to get out and then lifted the heavy latch on her own. "Now, let's use our dormant arm muscles and pull it back."

When the gate was open just enough to drive through, they breathed a sigh of relief and collapsed into fits of laughter. "I'm not looking forward to doing that every day," Cassie said after she caught her breath.

"Maybe Miss Winchester can buy an automatic door opener with our rent money. Let's bring it up when we negotiate." Diana grimaced.

"Negotiate? I thought you said the rent is only six hundred."

"Yes, but there are a few questions to ask: like getting an estimate for utilities, finding out if we can park in the garage, have guests or parties, and pets."

Diana put the gearshift into drive and continued up the road. As she approached the circular driveway, she slowed to admire the house and loved it even more.

Cassie put her hand on the steering wheel. "Stop!"

"What's the matter?"

"It's like something out of the *Addams Family*." Cassie peered up at the second story. "Half of those windows are boarded up; and what about the overgrown bushes under the windows? I can only imagine what lives in there."

"It has character, pure and simple. You're letting your imagination go off again."

"You and I have different ideas of *character*." Cassie pointed again. "Some of the shingles have fallen off. It must be real fun when it rains. What about mold and creepy things crawling up the walls?"

"We're living over the garage. Not in the house."

"Even worse!"

Diana drove toward the gas-lit portico. As an avid reader of romance novels, she visualized riding up on a dappled stallion and handing the reins to the handsome, young footman.

"I think we can park here." She shut off the engine and waited until an elderly man emerged from the house and approached the driver's side of the car. Diana rolled down the window and smiled. "Hello, I'm Diana Baker. We have an appointment."

He tipped his black cap. "Yes, miss. I'm Henry. You may leave your vehicle here. Miss Winchester is expecting you." He opened her door. "If I may show you the way."

"He looks eighty years old," Cassie whispered.

"Yes, thank you, sir." Diana winked at Cassie. "He's the chauffeur I told you about."

* * *

After spending an hour at the crash site, taking notes, and calling his assistant, John ate alone at the corner diner. Then he joined Chief Brady at the police station where the chief pulled two manila folders from a locked cabinet and placed them on the desk. "Would you like a cup of coffee before we look at these?"

John shook his head and held up his hand. "It's late. No more photos, please. I've seen everything I needed to see today." He swallowed hard. "I suspect you will disagree, but I'm positive Calvin isn't lying on the medical examiner's stainless steel table."

Chief Brady sat in his chair and leaned forward. "Sir, I understand how hard this is for you, but how could you possibly know that?"

John pounded his chest with his fist and struggled to keep from shouting. "I'm not delusional. He's alive. I can feel it. He may have been nabbed by bad guys. I might still receive a ransom demand. But I see the wrecked car and burned body as a general warning. I think it's about drugs."

Brady leaned back. "Drugs? Did your son use drugs or deal them on campus?"

John shook his head. "I'm not sure, but I have some experience about how these things go down. I believe he's being held incommunicado and the burn victim crossed them or was made an example." His resolve to stay in control crumbled and he decided to tell more. "There was another kidnapping on the same campus last spring and the innocent victim was a young man who ..."

"Yes?"

"What I'm about to tell you cannot leave this room. It's not about a crime, but a case of mistaken identity; it's about a man who lost another son twenty-one years ago, and of a father who wants to make it right."

"Go on, I'm a good listener."

John felt every ounce of strength leave his body. "I tell my clients it saves enormous time and trouble to tell the truth from the get-go. All things eventually come to light." He felt tears well in his eyes. "This is a story that is long overdue to be told, and I feel you can be trusted."

"But ..."

"Please let me continue."

John paced the room as he told Chief Brady about how he had been unfaithful to his wife on several out-of-town trips and how, on a particular one-night stand, he likely got his date pregnant. He took a break and sat opposite the chief, raised his hands as if in surrender, and slowly lowered them into his lap.

"I can't say that's the most unusual thing I've heard recently. My job is to question suspects and listen to victims' family members who are upset or mourning." The chief leaned forward. "I presume your wife doesn't know."

"Correct." John leaned back and stared at the ceiling. When he looked back at the chief, he felt the need to elaborate. "A short time after the encounter, this was over twenty years ago, I was contacted by the woman who told me she had become pregnant after our evening of partying and the inevitable roll in the hay. She wouldn't let it go." He ran his hands through his hair as if to rid himself of the memories.

"At first I thought she wanted money to take care of it, so I told her I'd pay for an abortion. She said that wasn't an option and demanded I leave my wife and marry her." He walked across the room and spoke to the window. "You can imagine how that went over." John's throat tightened. "I told her I would pay her medical expenses if she just went away. She sent me a few bills, and then I received a certified letter informing me her baby boy had been adopted. It didn't end there because she twisted the knife once more. His adoptive family lived in Naperville, Illinois, my home town. That was either a strange turn of fate or revenge. I'm going with revenge." He spit out his well-worn courtroom phrase, "I don't believe in coincidences. They are too convenient."

"So, this young man has no idea who his birth parents are?"

John shook his head. "I doubt it. But he could find out easily enough. Birth records are opened more than you know. Calvin was eighteen months old when Kevin was born, so they are close in age. Hell, they even attended the same high school and then crossed paths at Kent State." He sat and leaned forward. "You see, they look so much alike that the boys have already been mistaken for one another."

"Ah, the kidnapping on Kent State campus. I heard about that."

"Precisely. This matter is further complicated in that Glenn Baker, my law partner, is helping Kevin with the investigation. Kevin suffered broken bones, a concussion, and was left for dead in a hotel room - in Canada, no less. Kevin recovered from his physical injuries, but the doctors diagnosed him with short-term amnesia. He has since recovered. Now he wants answers. So far Glenn knows nothing about my relationship to Kevin."

As John continued his confession, the chief stood, poured a cup of coffee, and held up an empty mug. "Sure you don't want coffee?"

"No thanks, I'm about ready to head for the nearest bar. But first I have to book a hotel. Any suggestions?"

"I'll let my assistant help you with that."

John stood, headed to the door, and stopped. "I'm calling in my own detectives."

Chief Brady reacted. "We have the entire police department on this. We can handle the investigation."

"Nevertheless, I'm getting involved. I have to do something; either that or go nuts."

Chief Brady stepped forward and gripped John's shoulder. "I don't mean to sound harsh, but civilians have no business getting involved or impeding police procedures."

John pulled away. "Impede? Not to worry. I won't step on any toes." He yanked the door open and walked out.

CHAPTER 21
The Next Step

"THE LOGICAL THING TO DO is to cross Diana off the *People in My Life* list," Roberta told Zoë during their tarot card session the next day. "I'm glad your apprentice didn't show up. I'm not in the mood for having a stranger around."

"All for the best." Zoë shook her head. "Sad developments, my friend. You have been under so much stress. Dealing with people who add to it is counterproductive, bad for your aura. Unfortunately, this involves your daughter."

"You're loyal to the end, but Diana is *not* and has *never* been my daughter. The chickens have come home to roost and except for you and Charles, no one is on my side. Charles has no choice because he's my lawyer. Not that I can pay him in cash, only side benefits, if he's still interested." She chuckled.

"I'm a firm believer in positive thinking and will help you every step of this journey. Despite my gifts, I couldn't foresee my young son perishing in a bicycle accident. I understand the meaning of heartbreak."

"I remember ... it was a terrible time." Roberta leaned across the table and held her friend's hand. They sat in silence. When Roberta found her voice, it cracked with emotion. "So, now what?"

"We will work through this together." Zoë touched Roberta's forehead and smiled. "I know what you have been thinking. Running away again is not the answer."

"Maybe not. Even though it seems the easiest thing to do."

"The right thing is usually not the easiest. In fact, it rarely is." She retrieved her crystal ball from her medium's arsenal on the bookcase and held it above her head. "Herein are your answers. Let us begin."

* * *

After the reading, Roberta felt the need for a change of scenery to brush away the memories of what the cards and crystal ball had revealed. "Let's go for coffee. I have to get out of the house." Zoë agreed. They bundled up for the three-block walk to the neighborhood café. The gloom and mid-November wind that hinted of rain, maybe snow, hurried their steps. They found a small table by the window and hung their coats over the chairs. "This is my treat, Zoë. What would you like?"

"As much as I would love an espresso, given the hour, I'll have green tea."

Roberta returned with two steaming cups and a plate of warm cookies. "Couldn't resist." She poured an extra measure of cream into her coffee and looked at her reflection in the window. She touched the bags under her eyes. "I've aged ten years the last six months. It's been weeks since I've slept more than four or five hours."

"It's been a trying time for you."

"But with tonight's reading, you seemed to say, especially with the Fool, Magician, Strength, and Justice cards that I've been doing it wrong. But also you hinted there's hope, and a resolution isn't far away."

"If I'm wrong, then I am the fake you once accused me of being, but I believe I have interpreted the elements correctly."

Roberta used her spoon like a baton. "I believe you are a magician and have banished my troubles on the next flight to Timbuktu."

Roberta motioned for Zoë to lean forward so she could whisper, "I forgot to tell you. The cloutie came loose and dropped off the other day. I found it under the tree and it was all faded and torn. What next?"

Zoë sat back; it took her a moment to recover. "I knew Aurora's hanky would come through. Where is it?"

"Here." Roberta drew it from her purse and pushed it across the table.

Zoë picked it up, closed her eyes, and held the handkerchief to her cheek. "My dear, it means your wishes will come true." She opened her eyes. "But ..." Zoë held up her forefinger.

"You mean, there's good news and bad news," Roberta said.

Zoë shook her head. "Not exactly, but in due time answers will come about three-fold. So be ready for the unexpected." She paused. "Even with my and Aurora's gifts, we weren't able to curtail illness and tragedy in our own lives. Life doesn't *ever* work out perfectly."

She folded the hanky and set it on the table, then flipped her dangly earrings with a long red fingernail as if to change her mood. "So, you have something on the horizon and hopefully it will bring peace to your heart."

"Let's hope," Roberta agreed.

"I've been meaning to ask, is that a diary you've been carrying around?"

Roberta was surprised Zoë had noticed. "You caught me; either that or you can see through this ratty bag." She held up her well-worn, patchwork purse. "I remembered a while ago you said how journaling helps you keep sharp, more organized, so I decided to give it a try. Charles would be so proud."

"I'm happy you caught the meaning of my thoughts." Zoë placed a palm on her well-endowed chest. "The wise keep their deepest thoughts near-and-dear. I realize you don't believe in the power of prayer and call me a hypocrite when I pray, but a day doesn't pass without my alone time with God." She reached down and withdrew a pen from her purse. "I've used this fountain pen for journaling since college; it is always with me."

Roberta's left eyebrow arched. "College?"

"You seem surprised. Yes, I was a philosophy major with dreams to understand the world and then change it. But then life happened."

"Richie."

"Yes, I found myself pregnant with the little angel, but his father couldn't leave us fast enough. So I quit school and got a job. I was drawn to an herbal tea shop that sold candles and trinkets. There I met my mentor, Flora, and shortly after that Aurora joined the business. The rest is history." She spread her hands and then rested them in her lap.

Roberta sat back in surprise. "Philosophy major, tea shop, mentor. I've wondered how you got started as a medium. Guess that's why we became friends. My past is not so different."

"How so?"

Roberta relayed how her mother and grandmother had trained and then forced her to be a fortune teller, how they had traveled between fairs and carnivals, and eventually set up their home business. She left out her father, the beatings, neglect, hunger pangs, and heartache.

Zoë was moved to tears. "My dear. I had no idea you were coerced into doing things you hated." She dabbed her eyes with a white, silk hanky she always kept in her skirt pocket. "And at such a young age. How could a family member do such a thing?"

Roberta softened the tone of her voice. "Mama meant well, but she was under the influence of her mother, my nana. Anyway, cloutie aside, I need your advice. How should I handle this legal business with Diana's family, Glenn, the whole mess?"

"From twenty years of listening to the hurting, the desperate, and the lonely, I say *settle* with the family. Through your lawyer, lay it all out: your past mistakes, present circumstances, and let them decide whether you're worth a second chance." Zoë looked out the darkened window and appeared wistful. "Pray for forgiveness and then guidance. If the words don't come right away, or never, just tell God you want to make everything right. I know from experience, He listens and will answer, maybe not right away, but He will answer."

"Quite a speech." Roberta tapped the side of her head with her forefinger. "Repent and pray. As easy as that?"

Zoë smiled. "I have said all along, doing the best, the right thing is not easy. But your actions must be heartfelt, honest, and not rote as if from a script."

Roberta was beginning to feel uncomfortable and didn't want to venture into unfamiliar territory. "I'll think about it. Have another cookie?"

* * *

Diana and Cassie followed Henry into the great hall. "Please wait here while I announce you to Madam."

Cassie's mouth dropped open. "What a house. A basketball team could play in the entryway with room for a few fans. The ceiling must be twenty feet high."

"I told you, silly. This is a lovely place. Nothing to worry about."

"This way, ladies." Henry returned and motioned with his gloved hand as he led them into the parlor where a white-haired woman sat in a Queen Anne's chair.

"How nice to see you this fine evening." Miss Winchester rose to reveal her height, or lack thereof, and stood nearly a foot shorter than Cassie. She extended her hand in welcome. "You must be Cassie. I'm Miss Winchester, as you probably deduced."

"Yes, ma'am." She curtsied.

Cassie's gesture elicited a smile on Miss Winchester's part. "No need for formality, my dear. We're friends, plain and simple. Ah, Diana, good to see you again, and so soon. I am looking forward to having people living on the estate. It hasn't been the same since my nephew moved away. He had to fulfill family obligations in Amity, although I think he was looking forward to getting away."

Diana raised an eyebrow. "Getting *away*?" Diana twirled a lock of her hair and tried to dismiss the warning bell going off in her head.

"Poor choice of words. I meant to say, he was ready for a change. You know how restless young people can be." She fluttered her hands as if she had forgotten something. "Where are my manners? Please, have a chair and I'll ring for tea. Would you like tea, a cold beverage, perhaps?"

"Tea would be fine," Diana spoke up.

"Lovely." Miss Winchester tugged the embroidered rope with a silk tassel and in less than a minute, Henry appeared at the doorway. He bowed to show the bald spot on the top of his head.

"Where is Rose?" Miss Winchester asked.

"So sorry, Madam, but Rose received word about a family emergency and left a half-hour ago."

Miss Winchester touched her throat, her fingers fluttered, showing off her perfectly manicured nails. "My, I hope it isn't serious. Please keep me informed. Better yet, I will consult my tea leaves before bedtime."

"As you wish. May I be of service?"

"Could you serve us tea and brownies? And any other morsel left over from afternoon tea."

Henry put his gloved hands together in prayer fashion and bowed slightly. "Immediately, Madam."

"Thank you so much." She waved her hand with a flourish. "Now, girls, what should we chat about?"

Diana had gathered her train of thought and presented their questions about pets, having company, and the dreaded wrought iron gate matter. "I hope I'm not out of line in bringing these things up." She realized she had twisted her hair into a knot while talking and put her hand in her lap. Diana hoped she hadn't given a bad impression.

Miss Winchester motioned as if to dismiss their concerns; the movement allowed the lamplight to show off the gemstones on her left hand. "Nonsense. I am used to young people and their way of getting to the point. As for the kittens, they're welcome. The grounds have a variety of critters roaming about and I'm sure they will help keep the population down."

Cassie cleared her throat and gave Diana a *look*. Diana rolled her eyes at her friend and said, "Miss Winchester, they've been cooped up too long in our bedroom and will welcome the exercise."

"As for the front gate, we will work that out. I have been dependent on Henry and my nephew so I didn't see it as an inconvenience." She looked up as Henry re-entered the room with the refreshments. "Ah, Henry, thank you. Just set the tray on the table. I'll let the tea steep and pour in a moment.

"After our refreshments, I will have Henry take you for another tour of the garage apartment." She smiled at Cassie. "For your first visit, my dear. As for the timing, you may move in at your convenience. I only ask the rent be paid a month in advance."

"Yes, ma'am. I brought my checkbook so we can take care of that." Diana rummaged in her purse for a pen. "Sorry, may I borrow a pen? I seem to have lost mine."

"Surely. Just a moment and I'll retrieve one from my desk."

Diana watched her cross the room and admired her grace and timeless beauty. *She reminds me a little of Grandma Louise.*

"Here you are, my dear." Miss Winchester handed Diana an antique fountain pen. "Oh! I felt a spark. Must be a thunder storm on the horizon. Either that or we are soul-sisters. Do you do Ouija or consult a crystal ball perhaps?"

"Nooo, I'm not into the supernatural."

Miss Winchester settled down in her wingback chair. "Too bad. I will have to get out my crystal ball as soon as you are settled. It is most relaxing. She leaned forward and lifted the lid of the china teapot. "I think the tea is ready." She poured three cups.

Diana rose to accept the steaming cup of tea and noticed her hand was trembling. She took a deep breath and held out her palm instead. "Thank you. Lovely cups."

"The tea set belonged to my great-grandmother. My people emigrated from England hundreds of years ago." She set the bone china tea pot on the silver tray. "In fact, I believe a shirt-tale relative was condemned and burned as a witch in Salem, Massachusetts in the 1600s." Miss Winchester smiled. "Brownie anyone?"

* * *

Kevin wasn't prone to having premonitions, but he couldn't shake the feeling unusual events were coming, so when his phone rang late that evening and Diana's ID appeared, he wasn't surprised. "Hello."

"Kevin, I'm so glad I caught you. Do you have time to talk?"

He hesitated before answering, "Some."

"I was wrong not to call you back. Wrong, rude and I'm so sorry. *Please* come for Thanksgiving. Everyone will be here, and it would be awesome if you could meet my family. Cassie, too. I mean, not meet her, you already know her."

Kevin brushed her apology aside. "I've already decided to come. If you like I'll drive Buffy Bug out and bring Socks along for the ride." Kevin heard Diana catch her breath.

"I so don't deserve this. Thank you."

"No problem. There are some things to wrap up before I leave. I have to take another call, Diana. I'll be in touch." He clicked his phone. "Hello, Glenn."

"Kevin, I'm sorry to call so late. John Bergan phoned. He's in Kent, Ohio and asked me to take a couple days off and help out with looking into Calvin's disappearance."

"Are you going?"

"I'm leaving tomorrow morning, at ten." He paused. "Thanksgiving is next week so I plan to be back by Wednesday. Will you be in town?"

"No, I'm driving to Portland on Monday."

"Too bad. I was hoping we could get together. But I'm glad to hear you and Diana have made up."

"I wouldn't say that, sir. But I will need her car keys. She's okay with me driving it and her cat out."

"Fine. Stop by first thing in the morning, say seven. I'll have Socks ready. You'll want the pet carrier, too, or she'll be all over you."

"See you then. Good luck, sir."

CHAPTER 22
Change in Plans

JOHN AWOKE with a pounding headache and a hangover which threatened to cast a damper over the rest of his day. *Too much drink, not enough sleep. Glenn will be here in a few hours. Gotta get going.* He staggered to the bathroom, stuck out his tongue, and squinted at the mirror. "Great look you have going there, Mr. Bergan."

He turned on the shower to bring up hot water and gargled mouthwash to rid the stale taste of booze. John shed his wrinkled clothes onto the floor and eased under the hot stream before he remembered the bottle of Extra Strength Tylenol in his overnight bag.

"Damn." John threw the curtain aside, padded to the bedroom, tossed two capsules to the back of his throat, and swallowed hard. Back in the shower, he stood still and let the water cascade down his back. When he rotated his stiff shoulders, he felt knots of tension ease to a tolerable level.

Five minutes later, the cell phone rang from the depths of his pants pocket on the wet floor. He stepped out and picked it up. "John here."

"I'm still at O'Hare. My flight's been delayed due to a storm," Glenn said.

John sat on the edge of the tub and rubbed a towel over his wet hair. "Okay, keep me posted. I'm at the Hilton. Want me to reserve you a room?"

"I'd appreciate it."

"I'll see you when I see you." He tossed his crumpled clothes onto the bed, dried off, and then dug through his suitcase for a clean shirt and underwear. *Room service never sounded so good.* John ordered a light breakfast and when it came, he ate the fruit and wheat toast and guzzled a full pot of black coffee.

John's cell phone rang as he gulped the last drop. "Hello ... yes, Chief ... available? I'll be in town for a few more days. My law partner is flying in."

The troubled lawyer opened the sliding door to the patio, sat on a metal chair, and propped his feet against the railing. "What else have you discovered?" he asked.

"Nothing new. It will take some time to ID the b ... the victim." He heard the chief clear his throat. "You will be the first to know the results. Hopefully tomorrow."

"I've got the wheels in motion at my end," John said.

"We'll stay in touch."

He hung up and felt a wave of conflicting emotions wash over him and feared he wouldn't be able to get a handle on unfolding events. *I have to call Beverly. I've been keeping her in the dark too long.* He punched in his wife's cell number and prepared for an emotional conversation.

"Hello," Beverly said.

"Hon, I'm out of town and ..."

Beverly cut him off. "Surprise, surprise. I noticed the guest room bed hasn't been slept in for a while. Which bimbo are you with now?"

John felt his headache coming back. "Bev, will you listen for five minutes?"

"I'm so done with you and your lies."

"Don't hang up. It's about our son." John heard her sigh.

"Okay, you have my attention."

* * *

Diana and Cassie got in the car. Cassie slammed the door shut. "Ow, I twisted my wrist. Well, that was the strangest thing ever." She rubbed her wrist and held it up for Diana to see.

Diana saw Cassie's toddler-style pout and rolled her eyes for the umpteenth time that evening. "I think Miss W is the cutest thing, a little eccentric, but harmless. And what about Henry? He's like something out of *Downton Abbey*."

"I'm not worried about Henry. He's kind of cute for an old guy. But what's with the crystal ball and Ouija stuff? Salem witches. Too creepy. I thought you said you weren't into the supernatural."

Diana dismissed Cassie's remarks. "I'm not, but I'm trying to be open-minded. She's a sweet little old lady. She reminds me of Grandma Louise in looks. Remember Zoë, the fortune teller I told you about? Roberta's friend. She's a full-blown psychic and as harmless as herbal tea."

"Whatever. Do we have to go through with it?" Cassie slumped in her seat and looked out the window. "I'm sorry, but that house looks creepy. Correction, it *is* creepy."

"It's late. Everything looks a little scary at night." Diana started the engine. "I think it'll be fine, better than fine. Besides, we don't have anything else lined up."

"What's the rush?"

"I gave her the check. It's done."

"Technically." Cassie sighed. "Do you think it'll be a safe place for Wishin' and Hopin' to live?"

Diana backed the car out. "They'll be in kitty heaven."

"That's what I'm afraid of."

* * *

In Naperville, Kevin negotiated ten miles of slick roads from the tire store back to his home in the suburbs. He shook off snow from his hat and wiped his wet boots on the entryway rug. "Dang, I'm gonna hate driving in this stuff," he said to his dad, "but with new snow tires and the VW's rear-mounted engine, I should be okay."

"We'll worry the whole time you're on the road." His father finished tamping down the tobacco in his pipe and put the pipe into his pants pocket to use later.

"Shouldn't you re-think this? It would be best to travel in the spring. It's not like you and Diana are engaged or anything," Connie said as she approached from the kitchen.

Kevin hung his jacket and hat on the coatrack and rubbed his hands together. "What's for dinner?"

"Ham, scalloped potatoes, and green bean casserole," Connie said.

"Fantastic! Has Socks been behaving herself?" Kevin said as he leaned over to give his mother a kiss.

"I put her in the laundry room. You know I hate cats." Connie returned to the kitchen.

Richard shrugged his shoulders, patted Kevin on the back, and whispered, "Let's see if we can help your mother out with dinner. Maybe set the table." He raised his voice, "Here we come, dear," he called as they walked toward the kitchen.

* * *

Roberta called her lawyer at home that evening. "Charles, I need you to contact the Williamses as soon as possible."

"Why is that?"

Roberta balanced her phone under her chin, lit a cigarette, and paced her attic bedroom. "I've been advised to settle this once and for all. I can't go to trial. I wouldn't stand a chance."

"Advice? From whom? This isn't Las Vegas where you roll the dice and hope for the best. What's your bargaining chip?"

"I'm banking on them being decent people and accepting my heart-felt apology. They have Diana back. What more can they want?"

"Justice for their trauma and eighteen lost years."

"Ha, that's what Diana said." She heard a downstairs door slam and immediately threw her cigarette into the toilet, opened the tiny window, and turned on the fan. She knew Zoë's sensitive nose would smell the tiniest whiff of smoke.

"You haven't answered my question. Who have you been talking to?"

"Zoë." Roberta said and then winced.

Charles laughed. "So she told you to lay all your cards on the table. Of course, this was after she read your fortune and gazed into her crystal ball. Correct?"

"Something like that." Roberta groaned inwardly.

"Great. Let me work up something tonight. Come in tomorrow, say nine o'clock, and we'll talk it over."

Roberta hung up and then headed to the kitchen to tell Zoë the good news. She found her friend in the kitchen brewing a pot of tea.

"I phoned Charles and he's onboard with me reconciling with Diana's parents." She felt her neck prickle with the telling of another lie. *Is my conscience kicking in*? "We're getting together tomorrow."

Zoë held up her hands in apparent delight. "Wonderful! I couldn't be happier. How can we celebrate?"

"We can dive into that pan of brownies you have stashed in the pantry."

Zoë chuckled. "You caught me. I can't keep to my gluten-free diet like I should. Please get two plates while I pour the tea."

After she finished her first cup of tea and half of her brownie, Roberta had drummed up courage to discuss her deepest fear. She pushed her plate away. "Zoë, I need advice, maybe not advice, but reassurance."

Her friend leaned forward in obvious interest. "I'd be happy to help in any way."

"Let's set aside the purported powers of the cloutie, prayer, and good thoughts, where do we stand if I end up going to jail?"

"You mean as friends?" Zoë appeared confused.

"Yes. Will you stay in touch?"

"I feel so badly you had to ask. What is friendship? Is it something we take for granted and then cast aside when it's inconvenient or messy? I don't abandon my friends when they fall into bad times." She fumbled for her ever-present hanky and blew her nose. "I'm no judge. I don't throw stones; nor do I gossip."

Roberta felt a load lift and she shuddered in relief. "Thank you. I just needed to know where I stand, and if ..." She couldn't finish the sentence.

Zoë patted Roberta's hand. "You have enough on your mind. Please set aside your fears. You will never be alone, not as long as I draw breath."

CHAPTER 23
Against the Wall

THE THUGS HAD TAKEN CALVIN from his cell and set him in their common room. Calvin's arms were pulled crisscross behind his back and tied at the wrists. His calves were firmly bound to the legs of a heavy wooden chair. He struggled to sit in a more upright position to look one of his captors in the eye. "What do you expect to gain by holding me here? It's been what, a week? I'd like a shower. My three daily trips to the can and skimpy meals aren't cutting it either."

"How about we get some cooperation? Then we'll talk."

Calvin sneered. "I'd be happy to accommodate, if you'd clue me in. Seems like you're wasting everyone's time."

The burly man crushed his cigarette on the wood floor with an oily boot and scooted his chair a few inches closer to Calvin. "The Boss has been busy with people more important than you. But now he's ready to cut a deal with your old man." He leaned in. "I'll bet Daddy's ready to shell out big bucks to get your sorry ass home."

Burly sat back, lifted one cheek off the chair, let out a resounding fart, and laughed a hearty belly-laugh. "That's what we think of you." His crude actions spurred nervous laughter amongst his comrades.

Calvin knew he wasn't dealing with brain surgeons and he decided to play along. "Okay, let me call my dad so he knows I'm alive. He'll pay whatever you ask."

Burly scratched his bald head. "I don't think Boss Man will let you use the phone. Let me think on it a minute."

The skinny guy with a crewcut who was leaning against the brick wall pounded a fist into his palm. He chimed in, "We've wasted enough time. Let him give his daddy a sob story, but first let's make sure he has something to *cry* about."

Calvin's hands had been sweating long enough that he could wiggle his wrists a little. *Maybe if I loosen them enough, I can get untied back in my cell.*

"We gotta talk this over without him sitting here listening." Burley pointed to Calvin and then held his nose. "Besides, I can't stand your stink anymore." He stood and dragged Calvin, chair and all, back to his confinement.

He's a fine one to talk about me having a stink, Calvin thought as he suppressed a smile. Burly shoved Calvin against the wall under the window.

"Hey, how about taking off all these ties? It's not like I'm going anywhere," Calvin said. He held his breath as Burly appeared to consider the request.

"Can't hurt." Burley pulled out a menacing-looking switchblade, leaned over, and cut off the plastic wrist and leg ties, stuffed them in his pocket, turned off the light, and walked out.

Calvin waited until he heard the lock snap shut, then he glanced up, and calculated, I can stand on the chair, break the window with my elbow, and drop to whatever lies beyond.

* * *

Roberta sat next to the six-foot potted rubber tree and twisted the handles of her patchwork handbag in both hands. She craved her morning cigarette and cup of coffee. "It's after nine. How long will I have to wait?" she asked Charles' assistant.

Sandra looked up and smiled. "It shouldn't be long, Mrs. Baker. Would you like a cup of coffee? Two creams?"

Roberta nodded and looked out the window. "Great, on top of everything else, it looks like snow," she muttered under her breath.

Ten minutes later Roberta sat across from Charles; she felt cold chills run through her veins when he looked up from his yellow legal pad. "So, what did you come up with?" she asked.

Charles hesitated before he broke the news. "The D.A. will push forward with the kidnapping charge. Federal crimes don't get dismissed with a wave of a magic wand. And there is no statute of limitations."

"God." Roberta looked down and felt tears well in her eyes.

"However, the same hour the D.A. files the documents, I will work up a plea bargain claiming temporary insanity. The judge might reduce the charges and order a mental evaluation." Roberta opened her mouth to speak, but Charles held up his hand. "I can't guarantee this will work, but spending time in a psychiatric hospital is better than years in jail. Right?"

Roberta felt the room spin; she lowered her head and wiped her runny nose with the back of her hand. Charles opened a drawer and handed her a box of tissues.

"No matter what your card-shuffling, crystal-ball-gazing friend recommends, I will *not* contact the Williamses directly. We must go through proper legal channels." He leaned forward and folded his hands together. "Short-cutting this is not the best offense." He rose and walked around to Roberta's side of the desk. "I say *offense* because that's the method I choose to take. I don't think underdog, ever." He smiled. "Plus, I have my reputation to consider. Do we understand each other?"

"Yes." Roberta held her chin up and detected the hint of a threat in his eyes. She managed to smile back and thought about living in a psych ward, receiving free meals, cable television, being smarter than her idiot roommates, and garnering gifts and boatloads of sympathy from Zoë, maybe even Diana. "It could be a lot worse."

"Another shot of coffee before you head out?" Charles held up his empty cup.

Roberta sniffled, blew her nose, and stuffed two damp tissues into her purse. "No, I have things to take care of." She stood, squared her shoulders, and offered her hand to Charles. "Thank you."

"No problem." He walked her to the door and cracked it open. "Remember, no funny business. We need to stay in touch."

"I understand." Roberta slipped out and raced past Sandra as if her tail was on fire.

* * *

Diana stood and rubbed the small of her back with the heel of her hand. "I'm glad you don't have a ton of stuff to pack since most of your stuff is still in Boise. This is taking longer than I thought."

"Maybe that's because you're a major packrat." Cassie pointed to four boxes. "You have enough books to open a used bookstore." She threw her hands up in apparent frustration. "And clothes. Look at your closet."

"True, but we'll have two good-sized closets, tons of storage in the garage, and a cupboard for most of my books." Diana resumed stacking books into another box. "When is the rest of your stuff arriving?"

"Mom sent my things by UPS a couple of days ago. I should get a tracking number from her soon."

"Good. I know it's been hard for you living out of a suitcase," Diana said as she retrieved shoes and boots from the closet and tossed them into a bent-up box.

Cassie leaned over and tried to catch her kitty that was playing with scraps of newspaper used as packing material. "Got'cha, Wishy." She lifted the kitten up, scratched behind his soft, black ears, and kissed his wet nose. "How are we moving this stuff to the apartment?"

"Dad borrowed a utility trailer from Mr. Tabor, our gardener. It's plenty big."

Diana dropped a shoe to answer her phone. "Hello. Oh, Miss Winchester ... I'm fine, and you?" Diana raised her eyebrows, her eyes popped open. "The garage burned down?"

Miss Winchester continued, "Yes, dear. I don't know what happened. The fire department and police have been here. It looks like something electrical, but they are continuing their investigation." She paused. "I'm so glad you girls weren't living there. Can you imagine? I shudder to think." Diana thought she heard Miss Winchester choke back a sob.

"Gosh, how terrible. What was lost?" Diana's mind spun; her knees buckled and she collapsed onto the bed next to Cassie.

"The apartment furnishings, old Christmas lights and decorations, nothing of value. Thank goodness Henry left Lizzy out or I would have lost her, too. I guess things happen for a reason."

"Lizzy?" Diana was feeling more frustrated with Miss Winchester's confusing reaction to their dilemma.

"My Lincoln Continental. I've called her Lizzy ever since I bought her in 1990. A lovely car. So many memories."

"Ah." Diana rolled her eyes in frustration. "But we need a plan. Cassie and I are all packed and ready to move."

Miss W continued, "During breakfast, I had the most wonderful idea. Just a moment, while I sip my tea." Diana waited and focused on a piece of lint on the floor. Miss Winchester resumed, "I read my tea leaves and they told me to offer you rooms in the main house. I'm sure you and Cassie would be more comfortable, and your company would be most welcome."

Diana felt her heartbeats pound in her ears. "Live in the house with you?"

"I can't tell you how grateful I am my car wasn't burned up. Remember, *Driving Miss Daisy*?" Miss Winchester repeated. "Jessica Tandy was such a marvelous actress."

Diana gave in. "I think so; wasn't it about an elderly widow woman living in the South who had a black chauffeur and they became life-long friends?"

"Exactly; however, we're not in the South, Henry isn't black, but we had wonderful times in Lizzy."

Diana left the open-ended remark alone. "So, you want us to move into the main house? Won't you be put out?" She was trying to think of how to re-direct the conversation to the problem at hand.

"Not at all. The house is large, with many rooms. Remember the Bible verse: 'My Father's house has many rooms'?"

Diana wasn't wild about the reference to living in Heaven. She stood and wound between the boxes to stand at the window. "We *are* all packed and have a trailer ready to use."

"That's exactly why you should consider living in Bella Estate proper. In the meantime, I'll have Rose and Henry tidy up two of the best guest rooms. Goodbye until then." Miss Winchester hung up before Diana could answer.

Diana dropped her phone on the bed, looked at Cassie, and forced a smile. "Well, what do you think?"

Cassie rolled over. "I still don't like it, but it sounds like she's sealed up another done deal."

"It'll be fun. Just think, we'll be living in an honest to gosh estate in our own rooms, not over a stinky garage. Besides, she called the house 'Bella.' It means beautiful."

CHAPTER 24
A New Reality

JOHN BERGAN AND GLENN met for breakfast in the hotel's café two days later. Glenn opened the conversation, "I'm sorry for the delay, but considering the foul weather and long lines, it could have been worse."

John sipped his coffee and remained silent.

"It's still a few days before the Thanksgiving rush. All I saw were young people glued to their cell phones. They're probably college kids heading home for Mom's home-cooked meals," Glenn said.

John nodded, set down his cup, and poured ketchup on his scrambled eggs. He stirred them, took a bite, and flinched.

"I'm sorry you haven't received any news about Calvin. The waiting must be hell."

John finished chewing and wiped his mouth with a cloth napkin. "I haven't eaten in two days." He pushed his plate away. "They say no news is good news, so I'm trying to remain optimistic." He cleared his throat. "Beverly and I had our first good talk in two years. Unfortunately, it had to be over the phone. But I think it's possible this crisis could bring us back together. Lord knows we've been on the outs long enough."

"I sound like a broken record, but I am sorry." Glenn leaned back and scratched his newly grown beard. "I find Calvin's situation particularly disturbing. There are so many similarities with his disappearance and Kevin's abduction last year, I can't help but think there is a connection. I've learned to not believe in coincidences."

"Me neither. Glenn, I hope we can put aside our professional differences and join forces. Because when … when they find Calvin …" He waved his hand as if to dismiss dark thoughts. "I need to talk and I'd like you to hold tight before responding."

"You have my undivided attention." Glenn pushed his plate of pancakes aside.

John leaned forward and lowered his voice. "We still have no word on what happened to Calvin. The police expected some kind of contact by now, a ransom demand, evidence of foul play, solid clues."

John held his hands up as if in surrender. "It's time I fessed up, dropped the mask. What I'm going to tell you I've shared only with the police chief. I hate to admit it, but Beverly doesn't know this either. I haven't been honest with her for years. You may have noticed the strong physical resemblance between Kevin and Calvin; I believe that's why Kevin was mistaken for my son last year. The thugs made it right last week and abducted Calvin. Who knows why they waited so long?"

John relayed the truth of his affair and how and when he discovered the Wrights had adopted his natural son at birth. "I apologize. You may have been correct about Calvin's possible connection with drugs. I've been a terrible father and a worse husband. Beverly and I share the same house, but live separate lives. It's been going on for two, no three years now, but I don't want a divorce. I'm afraid if Calvin is dead, any chance of reconciliation will be gone. I can't face being alone."

"May I ask a couple of questions?" Glenn asked.

"Certainly."

"If Calvin is found alive, will you contact Kevin and acknowledge him as your son? And will you tell Beverly?"

John didn't flinch. "No matter what happens, I will tell Kevin the truth. And, yes, I will also tell Beverly. She can't be left in the dark. I'd like Calvin to know he has a brother. I've been torn apart by this for years. I haven't handled it well; I mean having two sons and not being able to acknowledge one." John sighed. "Maybe that's why Calvin and I aren't close. Funny, it wasn't very long ago I helped your Diana find her birth parents. Look how that turned out."

"If you mean my ex-wife is in serious legal trouble, Roberta brought it on herself. No sympathy there. But Diana is happy with her birth family, even though they have a lot of adjustments to make."

"I'll be making adjustments, too." Glenn took a sip of coffee to clear his head. "It's time for us to forget our differences. I will do my part to help you find Calvin. As for Kevin, I fully support your decision to contact him and tell him the truth. I love Diana as my own daughter, but there are times I wish I had a biological child. It's no small thing."

John seemed touched by Glenn's kind words. "Thank you. And I admit I was a real a-hole when I tried to pressure you to stop the inquiry into Kevin's kidnapping and assault. Maybe if I had done the right thing, Calvin wouldn't be ..."

"We will get through this," Glenn said.

John's phone rang. "Just a moment. Yes, Chief." He fell silent for a few seconds. "Say what? You found my son on the highway? How is he? Where is he?"

Glenn waited while John listened and repeated Chief Brady's news. "He was found walking along Highway 8, taken into protective custody, and is being checked out at a hospital. Where? I'll be there as soon as possible." John hung up, set his phone on the table, and appeared tongue-tied.

"Where is he?" Glenn asked.

John swallowed. "He's in Cuyahoga Falls, only twenty or thirty minutes from here. Can you believe it?"

Glenn smiled and slapped the table-top and knocked the cup off its saucer.

The waitress ran over to the table. "Is there something you need, sir?"

"Is it too early for champagne?"

* * *

Zoë was punching out bread dough when Roberta entered the kitchen. She wiped her sticky hands on a damp rag. "How did it go with your lawyer?"

Roberta sat on the kitchen chair with a *thud* and tossed her purse under the table. "As I told Charles, it could be worse."

"How so?" Zoë joined her friend and adjusted the drooping gerbera daisy in the table centerpiece. "There."

"When the charges are filed, Charles will enter a temporary insanity plea; and if I'm lucky, I may spend time in a mental facility. Any suggestions as to which one?"

Zoë sighed. "Oh, Roberta, I'm so sorry." She leaned forward and touched her friend's hand. "No time for dark humor. Let's try and stay positive."

Roberta snorted. "What will your cards say now? No more Grim Reaper? What about your crystal ball – has it given up on me, switched to another channel? I need a cigarette." She pulled her hand away and leaned over, scrounged, and found a bent one at the bottom of her purse.

"Go ahead, my dear. I will make an exception today. But let me brew a pot of healing herbal tea. It will calm your nerves and cleanse your system." Zoë waved her hands above her head, which spurred the tiny silver bells on her bracelet to tinkle. "Even my bells are spreading cheer."

Roberta's phone rang and she rummaged through her purse again. "Hello." She sat back and dropped her unlit cigarette on the tabletop. She nodded. "Yes, I understand. I'll be totally available. Talk to you soon."

Zoë lowered the gas flame under the teakettle and faced Roberta. "News?"

Roberta picked up the cigarette and with a shaky hand lit it with the silver lighter Charles had given her years before. She inhaled and held her breath for a second or two before she exhaled. "Charles received an email from the court. The original documents are in the mail. The hunt is on and I'm the prey."

Zoë retrieved two mugs from the cupboard, poured hot water into the ceramic teapot, and then dipped in a basket filled with fragrant herbs. "Now is the time to gather strength and invoke prayer and positive thoughts." She put her hands on her wide hips. "Ever tried yoga?"

"What the hell are you talking about? I need legal help, not flexible muscles," Roberta said.

* * *

"Okay, Cass, this is the last one." Diana shoved an overflowing box of shoes and purses into the bed of her father's truck and slammed the tailgate shut. The vibration knocked a couple of leather purses onto a box of books.

"See. You have way too much stuff," Cassie hollered as she opened the passenger door.

Diana climbed into the driver's side and adjusted the seat and rearview mirror. "I wish Dad was available to help us move today, but at least we can use the truck and utility trailer. We could have asked Bryan but he would have been more trouble than help." She smiled at Cassie and started the engine. "Here we go!"

Thirty minutes later Diana pulled into the drive leading to Bella Estate. "I'm glad Henry left the gate open. Let's hope he can help us unload."

Cassie shut the air vents on the front panel as they drove past the burned-out garage. "It still stinks." She pointed. "Just think we could have been asleep there when it happened."

"It smells bad alright. I wonder when it'll be torn down and cleaned up. Look, there's Henry. How did he know exactly what time we'd be here?"

"Miss W's tea leaves, maybe?" Cassie sounded sarcastic.

Henry was standing in the middle of the circular drive; he moved aside, tipped his driver's cap, and motioned them to drive to the side entrance. He followed and stood next to the truck as Diana pulled to a stop. "How nice to see you both again."

Diana opened the door and hopped down. "Thank you, Henry. Is it okay to park here for a while?"

"Yes indeed. Good fortune has smiled on us this week. My nephew, Reggie, is visiting so he can help carry up boxes, move furniture, store luggage and such. He's only fifteen, but strong for his age. I've been training him in the martial arts and he's close to earning his black belt in judo and taekwondo."

"We're ready to move in. Aren't we, Cass?" Diana saw Cassie's expression that bordered on resolution, not excitement.

Henry waved to a young man walking toward them. "Reggie, meet the girls, Miss Diana and Miss Cassie."

Reggie shoved his hands into his jeans' pockets, sauntered next to Henry, nodded to them, and muttered, "Hi."

"Nice to meet you," Diana said.

"Hello," Cassie echoed.

"Ready to get started?" Diana asked.

Reggie nodded and approached the back of the truck without being asked. Diana opened the truck's back door and pulled out one of the pet carriers while Reggie unlatched the tailgate. It fell with a loud *thud* which rocked the truck and made Diana jump.

Cassie ran over to rescue her kitten from the backseat. She opened the carrier door and cooed, "It'll be okay, Wishy, nothing's wrong." Cassie glared at Reggie, but he appeared disinterested in them or their cats.

It took forty-five minutes for Reggie and the girls to move their belongings into the upstairs bedrooms. "Thanks, Reggie, we couldn't have done it without you, at least not as fast." Diana held out her hand.

"Sure, no problem." He looked at Diana's gesture as though she was going to give him a tip and ignored the proffered handshake. "See ya' around." He slouched off and headed downstairs.

Diana chuckled. "He's strange."

Cassie raised one eyebrow. "I don't think he's wild about us moving in."

"I wonder why?" Diana mused.

Cassie fell onto Diana's queen-size bed, gazed up at the ruffled canopy, and sneezed. "I don't think they've vacuumed in months. And my bedroom smells musty."

"Maybe we can help out Miss W and do a little housecleaning. Might get a discount on the rent, too." Diana joined Cassie on the bed and ran her hand over the chenille bedspread. "Tickles. How's Wishy doing?"

"I left him in his pet carrier with a dish of water. There are too many places he can poke his head into and be lost forever. Have you checked out your closet?"

"No." Diana shook her head. "Why?"

Cassie hopped up, opened the double-doors, and peeked under the storage shelf. "I thought so. Come here." She motioned with her hand.

Diana looked inside. "Yeah, and?"

"There's an area just behind this shelf where you can stand straight and hide out." Cassie stepped in. "Like this. It's so dark, you can't see me."

"It's a deep closet for storage and stuff. Who'd want to 'hide out'?"

Cassie came out and touched the door. "What about these holes? Perfect for a peeping Tom." Cassie brushed off her jeans. "More creepiness."

"The holes are for ventilation." Diana stepped inside and looked around. "Or maybe the closets were used to hide spies during the war."

"Which war? The Civil War? The house might be old enough, but it isn't in the right part of the country, silly."

"I don't know and don't care." Diana came out and sneezed.

Cassie gave her a look, which seemed to say, "Told you."

"Everything will be fine, great," Diana said.

"If you say so." Cassie looked around. "Have you seen your kitty?" Diana shook her head. Cassie checked under the bed. "There you are, baby. Scared? Want to join Wishy in his kitty house? He's nervous, too." Cassie picked the kitten up and nuzzled its pink nose.

"Please, stop with the *scared* stuff or we'll have nightmares." Diana opened the window to let in fresh air. Hopin' broke out of Cassie's arms and hopped on the windowsill. "Watch over us, Hopin' and make sure ghosts don't creep up the side of the house."

CHAPTER 25
The End Game

CALVIN GRIPPED THE EDGE of the examination table and took deep breaths to clear his head as he waited in the curtained exam area of Western Reserve Hospital's busy Emergency Room. When his father came in, he started to stand. "Dad …"

"Don't try to get up." John approached the table and gave his son a prolonged hug. "I can't tell you how good it is to see you, son." He wiped a tear from his eye.

Calvin looked over his father's shoulder and saw Glenn standing inside the curtain. "Mr. Baker, you're here, too?"

"Wouldn't be anywhere else." Glenn walked over and shook Calvin's hand.

Calvin winced and rubbed his wrist.

"Sore?"

"Some. I was tied up the whole time and was plenty scared." He snickered. "But it was boring most of the time."

"Boring is good." John appeared to choke back a sob. "How did you get away?"

"When they told me they were ready to make a ransom demand, I told them I'd play along and call you. So I convinced them to cut my wrist and leg ties. After they left and locked the door, I made my move."

John pulled up a chair while Glenn stood motionless with his arms crossed over his chest.

"I stacked the bed cushions on a chair and climbed out the window."

"As easy as that?" John asked.

Calvin smiled. "Dad, these guys are really stupid. I listened to them argue about the dumbest things the whole time I was locked up." He looked at the floor for a moment, caught up in his emotions. "But I've been pretty stupid, too. And in some ways, I deserved what happened to me."

John appeared shocked. "What do you mean?"

"Even though I never hurt anyone, I did owe the boss man a lot of money. Two grand." He gave a wry chuckle. "My sins finally caught up with me."

"Son, I can help you take care of them. I know all the legal angles."

Calvin continued as if his father hadn't said anything. "I wanted to live in the fast lane and impress women, so I hooked up with people who convinced me I could make big money – no strings."

"Why, son? I sent you an allowance, you had a new car, school was paid for. You had no financial worries."

Calvin waved off his father's comments. "I know, Dad, but it wasn't enough. I ran up debts playing poker in a cardroom off campus so I decided to sell marijuana." He held his ribcage and succumbed to a coughing fit. Calvin caught his breath and managed to say, "I got in too deep and when I couldn't pay the suppliers or my IOUs, people started following me."

John didn't seem to react, so Calvin continued, "I was even mad at you for being a lawyer, you know, upholding the law. And remember when Kevin what's-his-name was kidnapped and beat up?"

John nodded. "An innocent person was put at great risk."

Calvin felt ashamed. "We look a lot alike. I think they mistook him for me. It's too late to change the past, but I want to make it up to Kevin."

"You will get that chance sooner than you think, son."

Calvin cocked his head. "Huh?"

"I'll leave you two alone. Catch you in the cafeteria, John," Glenn said.

An ER doctor entered the room just as Glenn passed through the curtain. He glanced up from his clipboard in time to avoid bumping into him. "Excuse me."

Calvin sat up straight and cleared his throat.

"I'm Doctor Rhodes." He stepped forward and shook Calvin's hand.

"I'll wait around the corner, son." John excused himself from the exam room.

"See you in a bit, Dad." Calvin took a deep breath and slowly exhaled in an effort to relax. He had always hated doctors, hospitals, shots, anything medically-related.

"I understand the police brought you in." Doctor Rhodes paused. "I mean they found you walking along the highway and brought you here."

"Yes, sir."

"Unbutton your shirt, please. Sorry, the stethoscope might be a little cold." The doctor examined Calvin, asked a few questions, and then invited John to join them. "Your son has given me permission to share this with you. I didn't find anything serious. However, he needs to take it easy for a while. He will be released as soon as the paperwork is complete."

"Thank you." John shook the doctor's hand.

Calvin waited until he was alone with his father. "I'd sure like to move home for a while, until I feel better."

"Your mother and I can't wait."

"How is Mom? Does she know?"

"She knows. But she's pretty upset. Mostly with me."

Calvin was confused. "Why?"

"I haven't been honest with her … in many ways."

"What do you mean?"

John put his arm around Calvin's shoulder. "Let's find your paperwork and get the ball rolling. While we wait for your discharge, I'll catch you up."

"The police will want to talk to me again."

"Yes, but first you're going to have a good meal and then we'll call your mother."

* * *

Roberta met with her lawyer the Monday before Thanksgiving. He started off on a positive note. "If the D.A. allows me, I hope to get this on a fast track despite the holidays. I'll request one of my favorite judges to preside over the hearing. We don't want a jury handling your case." Charles offered her an ashtray. "You can understand why."

Roberta had lit a cigarette on her way into the building and snuck by Sandra. She ignored the ashtray and stamped it out in Charles' empty crystal candy dish. "I'm not completely insensitive as to how this would look to the average person."

She leaned back in the soft leather chair, which was big enough to curl up and take a nap in. "I want to get my sentence started as soon as possible so I can be out by next Christmas. Is that possible?"

He laughed. "Holy hell, Berta, come back to the real world. The judge won't view one year as a fair sentence for a kidnapping and an eighteen-year cover up." He pulled a legal pad from his desk drawer and slapped it onto the desk. "Here are my notes, which I won't finish drafting until mid-December."

Roberta felt a surge of anger and stuffed it down. "Nothing I can do, I guess. So, when do you think my case will be heard?"

"After I finish detailing the facts, I will file a Request for Summary Judgment. I'll present your case as Temporary Insanity, which I am convinced is the truth. Remember when you told me you had a dream about a baby appearing on your bed; then you had an irresistible impulse to acquire a baby any way possible?"

Roberta hung her head. When she looked Charles in the eye, she said, "Yes."

"You took advantage of being a nurse which provided you with the perfect cover. Even though you fled town, you lived as if Diana was your own, with no tinge of remorse. You recall how I blew up at your warped logic and terrible actions?" Roberta remained silent.

"Okay, we'll go over a few more details before I complete my paperwork. After which, I will file the request. Then the scheduler will put it on the court docket. I know the calendar is full, so this will take time to rise to the top."

"Will I testify?"

Charles shook his head. "No, I hope to have a *hearing*, not a trial. If I can convince the D.A. to allow me to proceed, the judge will have everything he needs well ahead of time, including opposing counsel's arguments. He could make a decision right after hearing the verbal arguments."

Roberta opened her mouth to ask another question, but Charles continued, "It's possible we will have to wait a few weeks for his written opinion; hopefully this won't happen. The longer it takes for him to decide, the worse it could be for you."

"This could take months." Roberta lit another cigarette with a shaky hand and tossed the silver lighter into her purse. She winced. It had been a treasured gift, but today she hated the sight of it.

"Indeed, or perhaps a couple of years."

Roberta jerked her head up in alarm.

"Be prepared to put your life on hold. I mean no trips and no funny business."

"I'll be free to walk around, won't I?"

"You aren't under arrest, yet. I believe the court will view you as a minimal flight risk. You were in plain sight for almost two decades. However, the issue of bail is hanging out there."

Roberta dropped an ash on the carpet, but didn't move to pick it up. "This whole thing has become a friggin' nightmare. I just want it to be over."

"We're done for today. I'll have Sandra let you know after I've filed our response. Do you have access to a computer?" Roberta shook her head. "I usually email documents so you can print them off, but I'll instruct Sandra to drop them into the mail. Do we have your current address?"

"I'm not sure."

"Give it to her as you leave." He stood up.

"Meeting's over, I see." Roberta gathered her purse and stamped her cigarette into the candy dish. "I'll let myself out." She slipped out the door without her usual flair.

Sandra smiled as Roberta passed her desk, but Roberta ignored her and headed to the lobby and out the front door. For all she cared, they could keep their damned documents; she preferred to stay in the dark.

*　*　*

Kevin prepared to leave Naperville on a frosty Monday morning to begin the first leg of his two-thousand-mile drive to Portland. He placed ten CDs, five bottles of water, and a variety of snacks within reach. The backseat held Diana's not-too-happy cat stowed in her pet carrier between luggage and Christmas presents. Kevin's father made sure he had a couple of wool blankets in case of a breakdown or temporary road closures.

"Be sure and call us along the way," Connie said. He gave his mother a lengthy hug and assured her he would. Ever since his abduction, she had been clingy and paranoid about his safety whenever he left town.

Before Kevin turned the corner, he glanced in the rearview mirror and saw his mother on the porch with his father standing behind her. His father's hands rested on her slumped shoulders that looked weighed down with stress and worry. She didn't smile when he waved and gave them a thumbs-up, but she managed to blow him a kiss.

Kevin felt a twinge of guilt and hoped she would understand why he had to leave. He couldn't concentrate on studies until he settled matters with Diana. He didn't like the idea of Diana dumping him, and hated the idea of being alone. Kevin smiled remembering Cassie's up-beat personality and quirky sense of humor. He hoped her presence would cut the tension.

At the next stop sign, he flipped through the CDs on the passenger seat, and chose an album to match his mood. *What's better than a country-western break-up song?* Kevin knew he didn't have much of a voice, but he had memorized the lyrics to most of the songs and couldn't resist singing. He woke Socks and she meowed along. He chuckled and glanced over his shoulder. "Are you singing or complaining? Keep it up and we'll get along just fine, but you may get tired of me by the end of our trip."

* * *

Their first evening at Bella Estate, Diana and Cassie dined with Miss Winchester in the formal dining room. "Girls, I can't tell you how thrilled I am to have you staying upstairs. This old house takes on a life of its own at night. Your presence will be most reassuring."

Diana looked at Cassie, whose hand was frozen mid-air between her dinner plate and her open mouth. "What about Rose and Henry?" Diana asked.

Miss Winchester rang the silver dinner bell. "I don't wish to dismiss them as inconsequential, but their living quarters are on the first floor, way at the back. I don't see them as often as you would think. They have been here so long they tend to blend into the walls, rather like paintings." She smiled and popped a grape into her mouth.

"That sounds kind of strange," Diana managed to say.

Cassie choked, set her fork on the plate, and reached for a glass of water.

"I don't want to sound unfeeling, but when one has servants, one becomes used to them and doesn't think of them as people."

Rose entered the room. "Is there something you need, Mum?"

"May we have more rolls? The girls' appetites are heartier than I had anticipated." She held up her forefinger. "And please re-fill the water pitcher. Miss Cassie has developed a sudden thirst."

Rose curtsied and took the water pitcher and empty bread tray. "Yes, Mum."

"What was I saying? Oh, the kittens are most welcome. Feel free to let them roam upstairs and outside; however, not in the drawing or dining rooms, there are too many precious knickknacks to knock over."

Diana wondered how they could keep track of Wishin' and Hopin' when they were at school and work. The stairway from the second floor was open and if the kittens wanted to investigate downstairs, nothing would stop them.

"We'll do our best." Diana had lost her appetite and couldn't wait for the chance to retreat upstairs. It was their first night at Bella Estate, but Diana had a feeling Miss Winchester was going to get on her nerves and stay there.

"I know you will, dear. We will all get along just fine," Miss Winchester said.

A half-hour later, in the privacy of Diana's room, Cassie asked, "We won't have to eat with her every night, will we? I don't think I can stand it."

Diana shook her head. "I'll ask Henry if we can eat in the kitchen. I overheard him suggest to Miss W that we can either buy and cook our meals, or donate to the weekly budget. I'd rather chip in and then eat with the servants."

Cassie leaned back on the pillows. "I feel sorry for Henry and Rose. Miss W treats them like furniture. Boy, the garage apartment sounds like a dream now. We would have had privacy, with no moody teenager lurking around or Miss Creepy telling us bedtime stories."

Diana wanted their arrangement to succeed, but was having doubts. "If it doesn't work, then we'll move."

"In the meantime, what about our schedules?"

"Schedules?"

"You have Buffy Bug, or will as soon as Kevin brings it out, but I'll have to take the bus. You plan on driving me to the transit station, don't you?"

"Of course. Neither of us are morning people, so we'll have to work at getting up early." Diana's phone *pinged* and she pulled it out of her pocket. "Kevin just texted. He's on his way and is bringing Socks."

"Super. But he'll never find this place. Maybe we can meet him somewhere else."

"When he gets closer, I'll give him directions to my parents' house since that's where we'll be having Thanksgiving dinner."

"I should get back to my room. Don't know how well I'll sleep, though." Cassie got up. "Have you seen the cats recently?"

"No, but I'll look for them before I go to bed. Knock on my door in the morning and we'll have breakfast in the kitchen. I have to take Dad's truck back and clean up my old room."

"You may hear a knock on the wall in the middle of the night, but don't worry it won't be a ghost, it will be me letting you know I'm still alive," Cassie said.

CHAPTER 26
Birds of a Feather

WEDNESDAY EVENING Diana responded to Kevin's request for directions. She texted Kevin back with details and told her stomach to quit doing flip-flops. It was a long thirty minutes for Diana as she sat by the living room window and waited. Diana still felt tenderness and a sense of obligation toward Kevin; however, she had been barely seventeen when they met. After the first year, she realized her experience was the thrill of first love, puppy love, and not true, everlasting love.

When Diana saw him pull into the driveway, she called out, "Cassie, he's here."

Cassie rushed from the kitchen and skidded to a stop. "So soon?"

"He texted a half-hour ago from downtown Portland." She smiled. "You're excited, aren't you?"

"Yes, well, I mean, it will be nice to see him. It's been a long time." Cassie tugged at her short curls and bit her lip.

"Do you want to come with me?" Diana asked.

"No, you go." Cassie seemed embarrassed.

"I know he'd love to see you."

Cassie shook her head. "It wouldn't be right. I'll see him in a few minutes." She retreated to the kitchen where the rest of the family was finishing dinner.

When Kevin drove into the driveway, Diana went outside to meet him. She stood with her arms crisscrossed across her chest to stay warm. She watched Kevin step out, slam the door, and lean against Buffy Bug. His silence spurred her to leave the porch and approach the car. "Hey, Kev, I'm so glad you could come."

He cocked his head and smiled. "Thanks. You're looking good."

Despite the frosty air, Diana felt herself blush at the awkwardness of their reunion. "How did Socks do?"

"Great. We became good friends." Kevin pulled the pet carrier from the back seat and held it up. "Someone else is really glad to see you."

"Ooh, Sockies, baby," Diana cooed through the grate. Socks meowed and clawed at the door. "How was your ride, sweetie?"

"We sang together most of the way."

Diana laughed. "I would have loved to have been there." Kevin didn't respond. "Let's get inside. It's freezing," she said.

As they approached the house, Diana felt her eyes fill with tears, and she choked back a sob. Kevin stopped and looked directly at Diana. She paused and met his gaze.

He leaned over and gave her a hug. "What happened to us?" he asked.

His winter coat muffled her sniffles. "Oh, Kev, I feel so bad. But we can't talk about it now. Everyone's here and can't wait to meet you." She pulled away, raced up the steps, and led him inside.

Diana's family was waiting for them in the living room. Her father extended his hand in greeting. "Good to meet you, Kevin. I'm James, Diana's father. How was the drive?"

Kevin set the carrier on the floor and shook James' hand. "Not bad, sir, lots of rain, some snow, but I didn't have any trouble."

"Fine, good to hear. Here's the rest of the family." Everyone exchanged introductions and pleasantries.

"I'll be right back." Diana excused herself to take Socks to the laundry room where she let the kitty out of her plastic prison; Socks jumped out, brushed against Diana's leg, and purred. "Wish I could stay with you." She picked her up and snuggled the kitty against her cheek for a moment and before setting her down she said, "Here's your food and water, sweetie, you must be hungry. I won't be long, promise."

She entered the hall and heard Kevin protesting her parents' offer to stay at the house for the rest of the week. "No, really, I was thinking of staying at a hotel."

"Nonsense, we have a spare room in the basement. Well, it's not really a basement, more of an unfinished party room," James said. "I wouldn't feel right knowing you're by yourself during the holiday weekend."

"Absolutely, you must stay with us," Emily agreed.

"We'll help you unload the car. Bryan, then you can show Kevin to his room and help him carry his luggage downstairs," James added as he headed outside.

"Will do!" Bryan said.

Kevin looked embarrassed. "I appreciate your generous offer, thank you." He turned to Bryan. "Ready? Let's unload the car."

* * *

Roberta and Zoë had been up since 7 a.m. preparing their Thanksgiving meal. "Berta, I will be here for you no matter what happens."

Roberta smirked. "I just hope I won't be in the mental hospital too long."

Zoë dropped her potato masher into the mixing bowl. "Oh, I certainly hope not."

Roberta shrugged. "It sounds a whole lot better than prison."

"Don't fret, I'm sure Charles will convince the judge you meant no harm. I mean, that you temporarily lost your mind." Zoë returned to mashing the potatoes, adding warm milk and several pats of butter to the bowl.

Roberta winced at the 'lost your mind' comment. "Will we be stuffing the turkey?"

"Yes, I think the dressing tastes so much better, and the turkey doesn't seem as dry."

The doorbell rang. "Whoever can be coming on Thanksgiving Day?" Zoë wiped her hands on her apron, took it off, and headed to the entryway.

Zoë opened the door to find Claire Donnelly, the owner of Second Time Around Antiques and Roberta's former employer, standing at the front door. "Mrs. Donnelly, what a nice surprise. Please, come in."

She stepped inside. "Thank you. I assume Roberta is here."

"Yes, indeed." She called over her shoulder, "Roberta, Mrs. Donnelly is paying us a visit."

Roberta dropped the pie dough on the counter and scurried to the living room. "Claire, what are you doing here?"

Claire looked at the floor and then directly at Roberta. "I hate to bring you bad news on a holiday, but Clay and I are heading out of town for a few days and I need to tell you what has happened."

"What?" Roberta asked.

"A detective came to our door a couple of days ago. He asked us questions about you and brought up things so shocking. Let me say, I didn't know how to respond."

"Please, let's go to the sitting room, Mrs. Donnelly," Zoë said.

Roberta sat in the red velvet chair and wrung her hands in distress. Claire chose the tufted green chair and looked around the room. Zoë remained standing at the doorway.

"You can speak in front of Zoë. She's my spiritual guide," Roberta said.

"That explains the astrological signs painted on the wall. Then you're a fortune teller?" Claire asked Zoë.

"I don't like the connotation of 'fortune teller.' I prefer psychic consultant or as Roberta said, *spiritual guide* or advisor, if you prefer."

Roberta cut in, "Claire, what do you mean? A detective came to your house?"

Claire spread her hands up and outward. "This huge man showed up at our door and he seemed to know an awful lot about you and your past. The things he implied were shocking."

Roberta felt a wave of nausea wash over her. "What was his name?"

"Stan something. He was so imposing, he took my breath away when he appeared at our shop. I didn't think he was a real customer."

"He was a big, black guy, right?"

Claire nodded. "Yes. He wasn't offensive or threatening, but his physical size made me feel uncomfortable, and ..."

Roberta interrupted, "I can't believe this. Well, actually, I do. I've met him."

Claire continued, "If you've met him, then you know his manner. To us he was polite, but persistent. He asked us if we knew you were a kidnapper and under investigation. Roberta, what is going on?"

Roberta let out a deep sigh. "Because we've been friends for so long, I can trust you with the truth. I took Diana from a hospital nursery and kept her as my daughter for eighteen years. But she's been reunited with her family."

Claire gasped. "Roberta, how dreadful." She rubbed her forehead. "You must be in deep legal trouble."

"Yes."

Claire bowed her head and appeared to need time to absorb Roberta's confession. She looked up. "What happens next?"

"Charles, my lawyer, will file a request for a hearing in front of a judge. He wants to avoid a jury trial." Roberta felt dizzy. "It will take some time, but it's possible I could be put away."

"In jail?" Claire's eyes opened wide.

"I hope not. Charles says it's more likely I'll serve time in a psychiatric facility of some sort. Where, I don't know." She shook her head and looked away.

Claire looked incredulous. "This is terrible. The worst thing imaginable. I'll have to talk it over with Clay. We've come to count on you working part-time at the store, but if you will be distracted, or worse, we'll have to make changes."

"I'm fired?"

"Well, you were gone for several weeks, so I hired a high school girl who comes in after school. She's working out fine."

Zoë cleared her throat and said, "I can vouch for Roberta's change of character. She understands what she's done and what is at stake now. She is putting her priorities in order."

Roberta watched Claire for a reaction, but she remained stoic, as if in shock or so upset she didn't know what to say.

"If you could find it in your heart to let her come back, I know she would be most appreciative," Zoë pressed.

Roberta's shoulders slumped in relief, and she smiled at her friend.

Claire stood. "We'll see. I have to go. We're heading to Seattle to spend the next few days with our daughter." She looked at her watch. "I'm way behind schedule as it is. Roberta, I'll get back to you when we return."

"Thank you for coming over. I'm sorry for the fuss. I'll keep you posted and promise not to hide anything." Roberta walked Claire to the door. "May I give you a hug?"

Claire let Roberta lean toward her and accepted her embrace; however, she didn't return the gesture. "We'll be in touch. Have a nice Thanksgiving, Roberta. Zoë, thank you for your hospitality." She opened the door; the cold air added to the chill in the room.

CHAPTER 27
Turkey Day

DIANA'S FAMILY AND GUESTS gathered around the dining room table. The twins had decorated it with a festive centerpiece, china and silver place settings, and crystal stemware on an ivory linen tablecloth. It was 7 p.m. and their Thanksgiving dinner was two hours behind schedule. The oven hadn't cooperated and James tinkered with the circuit breaker three times.

"Let's give thanks for this wonderful meal." James asked them to join hands while he gave the blessing. He no sooner said, "Amen" when Bryan grabbed the spoon to dish up mashed potatoes.

"Bry, where are your manners? We are going to pass the food around the table. But guests will be served first," Emily scolded.

"I'm starving," he protested.

Kevin, who was sitting next to Bryan, leaned sideways and whispered without moving his lips, "I used to get into trouble for tossing rolls across the dinner table."

Bryan smiled and offered Kevin a fist-bump.

Diana sat across the table from Cassie and watched her steal sideways glances at Kevin throughout dinner. She smiled inwardly, pleased to see Cassie appearing hopeful and happy. Diana was rooting for them to become a couple; however, she suspected Kevin had driven two thousand miles to re-boot their relationship. He wouldn't make a play for her best friend.

"Kevin, it was so thoughtful of you to bring Diana's car and kitty all the way out from Illinois, especially in this weather," Emily said.

He swallowed a mouthful of gravy-drenched dressing and wiped his mouth with his napkin. "No problem, ma'am, I have the time and I've never been to Portland."

"How long will you be in town?" James asked.

"I have a flight scheduled for next Wednesday."

"Don't classes begin on Monday?" Diana asked.

Kevin frowned. "Remember, I'm a junior. Most of my courses are under my belt. My classes resume Tuesday night. I can afford to miss one or two." He reached for his glass of wine and took a gulp.

Cassie cleared her throat. "We'll have time to take Kevin to meet Miss Winchester."

"Who's Miss Winchester?" he asked.

Diana explained their relationship to Miss W and then gave a brief description of the house and its location. "She's eccentric, but sweet in a grandmotherly way."

"Eccentric? I think she's a nutcase," Cassie said.

"You're exaggerating." Diana rolled her eyes. "Miss W might be a little out of touch, but she can't help it. Except for two servants and a gardener, she's lived alone for years."

"But her nephew stayed with her while he was in high school," Cassie said.

"Yes, but she said he was gone all day with school and a part-time job. The house is secluded and she only gets out when Henry drives Lizzy."

Kevin raised his eyebrows. Diana hastened to say, "Lizzy is her Lincoln Continental. Henry is her butler and chauffeur, plus he's a martial arts expert. I guess you could say he's a body guard, too."

"Why didn't you choose a place closer to town?" Kevin asked.

Diana didn't want to get into a discussion over dinner. "We tried, but couldn't afford a place in the neighborhoods we liked. It'll work fine until something else comes along."

"Sounds sketchy to me, but it's your life," Kevin said.

"It is," Diana muttered. She resented his implication they had made a bad decision and decided to steer the conversation. "Let me know when I can help you serve dessert, Mom."

Emily looked relieved. She stood. "I think we're ready. Bryan, please help clear. Kerri and Kate, can you load the dishwasher while Diana and I cut the pies? We have pumpkin and cinnamon apple, and melt-in-your-mouth butter tarts. Cassie, Kevin, the family recipes have been handed down for generations and are Thanksgiving and Christmas traditions." She smiled and disappeared into the kitchen.

"I can eat six butter tarts in five minutes." Bryan rubbed his stomach, picked up his dishes, and headed to the kitchen.

After Bryan left to join the women, James leaned forward. "Cassie, I've been watching you two and have a feeling you and Kevin know each other."

Cassie nodded. "Last summer Diana and Kevin stayed with Mom and me for a few days. It was a big help because Mom was going through cancer treatments."

"Cancer, how terrible. How is she doing?"

"She's in remission and flew to Illinois to spend Thanksgiving week with Diana's father," Cassie said.

"With Glenn? The plot thickens." James chuckled.

"I guess I can tell you. Mom and Glenn are engaged, or will be by Christmas."

James slapped the table. "Wonderful. Diana will have another sister."

"We're pretty excited," Cassie said.

James said, "So, Kevin, you drove all the way from Naperville to Boise to visit Cassie and her mother? That's quite a road trip you embarked on."

"We stopped in Boise on the way home from Astoria, Oregon where we saw ... after we spent a day with Roberta," Kevin said.

James raised his eyebrows. "Astoria? I thought Roberta lived in Boise."

"It's a long story, but when we found out Roberta skipped town, Diana decided to confront her about whether she was her birth mom or her kidnapper."

James held up his hand. "I get the picture and can only imagine how things went."

Kevin shook his head. "It was awful. Roberta was horrible, mean, and nasty. She treated Diana like she was garbage and pulled a gun on Big Stan."

James appeared shocked. "Pulled a gun on ... who is Big Stan?"

"I'll give you the short version. Stan Hathaway is an ex-cop turned P.I. who works for Glenn. He's also psychic, I mean, he has a way of sensing things, and when he told Diana Roberta split town and she might do something desperate if we didn't intervene, the three of us flew out."

"I had no idea. The more I learn about Roberta, the angrier I get and the more confused I get."

Kevin nodded. "There's a lot of confusion surrounding Roberta. I was so mad at her, it took me a while to call the woman by her first name. I had plenty of others in mind." He held up his wine glass for a re-fill. "Remind me to tell you how Big Stan helped save my life."

"I'll hold you to it." James poured wine for himself and Kevin and raised his glass. "To you, Kevin, and to Cassie and her mother. What's her name, dear?"

"Maggie," Cassie said.

"To Maggie and Glenn. We'll make a toast to the whole family when the rest join us for dessert."

Cassie set down her glass of sparkling cider. "I'll see if they need help. What kind of pie do you want?" she asked the men.

"Pumpkin, but no whipped cream. Thanks," Kevin said.

"A small slice each of apple and pumpkin with plenty of whipped cream and a butter tart, please." James waited for Cassie to leave the room. "Now, tell me how Big Stan saved your life."

* * *

Roberta and Zoë sat in the rarely-used dining room and enjoyed the traditional fare of turkey, dressing, mashed potatoes, and green bean casserole.

"This is so delicious. Thank you for helping. I know cooking isn't your thing." Zoë sipped the last of her sparkling cider, set it down, and then tapped her long, red fingernail on the rim of the glass. "I hope Claire didn't ruin your day when she told you about Stan dropping by their store."

Roberta leaned back and loosened her belt. "I'm disappointed Claire and Clay listened to that creep. I thought we were friends." Her hand twitched. She craved a post-meal cigarette. "Stan works for Glenn. I wonder what they're planning next."

"It's all so unfortunate."

"I call it a conspiracy. I'm outnumbered. This will be one hell of a ride the next few months." Roberta stood. "I need coffee. Are you ready for dessert?"

"Yes, I'm looking forward to eating your first try at baking a pie."

Roberta took her dishes to the kitchen. She raised her voice so Zoë could hear, "I hope this legal mess won't force me to move out."

Zoë joined Roberta in the kitchen. "What makes you think I would ask you to leave?"

"A feeling I have. I know you hate discord and messed-up auras, and how it ruins the delicate atmospheric balance around here." Roberta waved her hands around.

"We'll manage. I have an unbreakable rule. I don't abandon my friends when they are going through tough times." She rummaged through the pantry. "I'm looking for rum to add to our coffee. Sound good?"

"I'll get mugs, the big ones."

"After dessert, let's move to the reading room so I can bring out the crystal ball and cards. It's been a while since you've had a thorough reading."

Thirty minutes later, Zoë and Roberta sat in the room infused with licorice incense, taped flute music, and candlelight from two dozen candles of various sizes. "I'll shuffle and then please cut the cards as usual, Roberta."

Roberta did so and set the stack in the middle of the table. "I'm curious. Why do you use cards and a crystal ball? Can't you just hold my hands and gaze into the great beyond to see the future?"

Zoë pressed the deck between her palms before she flipped several cards face-side up and formed the traditional Celtic Cross configuration. "There are exceptions, but I use the cards as a grounding tool to serve as interpreters to the unseen world. They also reveal patterns with repeated sessions. Over the years, I've learned to recognize those patterns and translate them." She bowed as if in prayer. "I must concentrate."

She remained silent for a few moments before she pulled three cards aside. "You will be dealing with legal troubles for a while."

"Tell me something I don't know," Roberta said.

Zoë appeared to ignore the snarky comment. "I see someone who could add to your troubles, make your life more complicated."

"Who?" Roberta gripped the edge of her chair.

"Remember back to when this trouble began, and how I warned you of an imposing man with dark hair?"

Roberta nodded. "How can I forget? You keep bringing him up. But at first I thought you meant Glenn."

Zoë looked up. "I believe it is Stan, the gentleman who appeared at Claire's store."

"Don't say *gentleman* and Stan in the same sentence. He's caused too much trouble already." Roberta had been careful not to tell Zoë about their altercation in Astoria because she had lied to her friend about why she left town in such a hurry.

Zoë sat back and pushed her long, wavy auburn hair away from her face. "You cannot ignore his presence. This man has re-entered your life for a reason. You must be prepared to deal with him."

"Prepare how? I want advice, not warnings and vague threats," Roberta said.

"I should only tell you what I see." Zoë pushed the three offending cards aside and drew three more. "Be patient. All is never revealed in the first pass."

Roberta breathed slowly. It would take all of her willpower to remain calm during the entire session.

* * *

Big Stan sat in an empty 24-hour Boise diner on Thanksgiving night. The turkey was dry and the dressing was tasteless, but he'd eaten worse. He preferred being on the road during the holidays. His empty apartment harbored too many memories.

Stan drank coffee and scrolled through his iPhone, checking football scores and messages. He smiled when he read one from Diana which wished him a happy Thanksgiving. Glenn's text said, "You need and deserve a vacation. See you in a week or two. Happy Turkey Day, buddy."

"More coffee?" the server asked.

"Yes, please, and some pie. Whatever you have left," Stan said.

She returned with two pieces on a dinner plate and a side of vanilla ice cream. "We won't be selling more pie this late. I'll only charge for one." She flashed a tired smile.

Stan picked up his fork and saluted. "Thank you, much appreciated." He looked around. "Seems like I'm the only one eating out tonight. Sorry if I'm keeping you from family."

"I only have a cat." She smiled. "A Persian I call Queen Latifa. She's a handful."

Stan chuckled. "Great name. Pets are a comfort. I'm away from home so much it wouldn't work for me to have one."

"You're not from around here?"

"No, ma'am, back east, the mid-west to be precise."

"Welcome to Boise, such as it is."

"Every town has its good and bad. Me, I've been in worse. Come Thanksgiving or Christmas you don't want to be by yourself in New York City or Chicago. The crowds make ya feel more alone."

"Really? I didn't introduce myself. I'm Inez."

"Nice to meet you, Inez. I'm Stan."

"What brings you to our city?"

Stan leaned back. "I'm running an investigation."

"Who'd make you work over Thanksgiving?"

Stan shook his head. "No one, it was my choice. An innocent young girl has been done wrong."

"That's dedication."

Stan took a bite of the warm blackberry pie. "Mmm. This tastes a whole lot better than the turkey and dressing."

Inez shook her head. "Sorry. The regular cook called in sick and his assistant doesn't know squat. I'll only charge you for the pie."

"Don't want you to get into trouble with the boss."

"I won't. My brother-in-law runs this place. He's a good guy. I best get to the kitchen and help Frank with a few things. Hope you find what you're looking for."

"I always do. Thanks again."

After he polished off his dessert, Stan left Inez a twenty-dollar tip and headed to his hotel.

CHAPTER 28
The Day After

DIANA WOKE THE NEXT MORNING with a pounding headache. She rubbed her eyes to focus and saw Cassie asleep in the other twin bed. Diana faced the wall, pulled the covers over her head, and played last night's repartees through her mind. Her cheeks burned with the memory of Kevin making curt remarks in front of the family.

Diana wanted to buy time before she and Kevin had their heart-to-heart talk and hoped the family would split up to shop, watch football, eat leftovers, or nap. Her wish came true when Emily brought up the subject at breakfast.

"Who wants to battle the crowds for some great deals?" Emily asked.

Four hands went up in a gender-split. The women voted to shop Black Friday bargains which left the men to fend for themselves.

"The van leaves in a half-hour. We're already way behind the early birds." Emily asked, "Bry, will you and Dad clear the table and tidy the kitchen?"

Bryan grabbed his cereal bowl and jumped out of his chair. "How about Kevin helping, too?"

"Sure. I know how to do dishes," Kevin said.

"No, Kevin is our guest. Make yourself at home, dear." Emily patted Kevin's shoulder as she went by.

A few minutes later, Kevin caught Diana alone in the entryway while she put on her coat. "Di, we have to talk. I didn't drive all this way to be brushed off."

"You sounded pretty rude last night. And it's none of your business where Cassie and I live." Diana shoved on her gloves. "Did you expect me to discuss our problems over dinner and ignore the family for the rest of the evening?"

"Maybe. Everyone knows I came to see you."

"I'll be back later this afternoon. We can talk then." She started to leave.

"Never thought I'd say this, but you're a coward, Diana."

She clenched her hands. "I'm not, I mean, I don't want to hurt you. You've been through so much."

"I see. All you have left is pity, not love." Kevin crossed his arms over his chest and leaned against the closet doorjamb.

Diana faced him. "I loved you and I still care about you, but I was only seventeen when we met. I was going through a terrible time with Roberta. You had your accident and months of rehab and most of the time we lived two thousand miles apart. Life got in our way." She felt backed into a corner. "This isn't the time or place to talk."

Kevin reached for her hand. "Wait. I'm not mad at you, but I'm trying to understand what happened to us. Remember the tattoos we got?" He held out his arm and pointed to the tattoo of a tree trunk with their initials.

Diana looked at his arm and whispered, "I remember. I see my heart tattoo every day."

Cassie came around the corner from the kitchen. "Diana, we need to ..." She stopped when she saw Kevin and Diana holding hands.

Kevin released Diana. She removed a glove and wiped her eyes with her hand. "We need to do what, Cass?"

"I'm sorry to interrupt, but we have to check on the kitties. They've been cooped up in our rooms for two days."

"They have plenty of food and water, and their litter boxes should be okay." She took a deep breath. "But you're right. Kevin, want to go with us?"

"Sure, I'm curious about this mysterious place you call *Home Sweet Home*."

"We'll be back no later than three and then we'll head over. Let's get going, Cass. Mom's probably waiting for us in the garage. She's anxious to get some Christmas shopping done. I am, too."

Diana tried to enjoy their shopping trip, but visions of her and Kevin fighting kept popping up in her mind. She couldn't wait for the week to end so she could get back to living the life she was beginning to get used to.

Maybe I'll just wallow in bed with Mom's desserts and my favorite books when I get home.

* * *

Big Stan left the hotel and drove his rental car to Zoë's. He expected Roberta to be hostile, and she was not obligated to talk to him. However, he had lingering questions regarding the facts surrounding Diana's kidnapping. His concern for justice for Diana trumped his concerns of overstepping standard investigatory practices.

Zoë answered the door within seconds of Stan ringing the bell. "Yes?" She appeared composed; however, she kept the storm door locked and held the interior door open a few inches.

He noticed her knuckles were turning white. He tipped his winter cap in greeting. "Ma'am, I'm Stan Hathaway and I understand Roberta Baker lives here."

"Maybe."

"If she's available, I'd much appreciate it if I could talk to her."

"Perhaps another day." She started to close the door.

Stan glanced to the right and saw the signage, Madam Zoë's Psychic Readings & Spiritual Advice by Appointment Only: 208-555-4236.

"Could you give her my card so we can touch bases before I head out of town?"

"You may leave it on the doormat."

Roberta came up behind Zoë. "Did I hear my name?" She saw Stan and uttered a few adjectives and expletives, which oddly came out in alphabetical order.

Stan tipped his hat again. "Mrs. Baker, I'm ..."

"I know who you are. I haven't forgotten our first meeting when you and that smart-aleck boy snuck up on me. How dare you come to my home?"

Stan took a step back to send the message he wasn't a threat. "I was in town on other business and thought I'd stop by. I won't need much of your time."

"B.S., you went to my employers' store the other day and spread lies about me. How dare you come here? Get lost."

"I won't push it." Stan quickly formed an idea and addressed Zoë, "Ma'am, I noticed your sign and would be grateful if I could make an appointment for a reading while I'm in town. I sure could use some sage advice."

Zoë opened the interior door a little farther. "Goodness, I never turn away a client. But just a moment and I'll look at my schedule and see what I can do."

"Good grief, don't you see what he's doing?" Roberta snarled.

"Dear, how would you feel if I refused to see someone in their hour of need and then he did something desperate?" She asked as she closed the door.

Stan stomped his feet on the mat and rubbed his gloved hands together to keep the circulation going. In less than five minutes, Zoë opened the interior door and unlocked the storm door.

"Please, enter. I find I have an extra hour. However, I will not permit you to talk to my friend."

"Understood. Thank you, ma'am." Stan entered and waited in the vestibule while Roberta clomped upstairs. Stan watched her exit and heard muted cursing before a door slammed shut. It was like watching a one-woman train wreck. He couldn't help himself.

Zoë appeared to ignore Roberta's exit and waved her hand to the right. "Please have a seat in my parlor. I'll only be a moment."

Stan entered the room whose only light came from the fire in the fireplace, took off his hat, coat, and gloves, and chose the velvet-tufted armchair by the hearth. He draped his coat over the back of the chair and inspected the room with the eye of a trained law enforcement professional. He felt his heart rate slow down and the tension in his neck muscles begin to loosen. It was as if he was sitting in his Boston home with his wife and son just a room away. He closed his eyes and let the fifteen-year-old memory wash over him.

Zoë reappeared carrying a gold silk tablecloth, her crystal ball, and a pack of cards. "Please join me at the table."

Stan woke from his reverie and stood abruptly. He quickly recovered from a sudden dizzy spell. "Let me give you a hand."

"Thank you, no. I'd rather arrange the reading table myself." Zoë placed the crystal ball, cloth, and cards on a footstool and then removed the Tiffany-style lamp and a bowl containing crystal nuggets from the table. "Because of the holiday, I have time to read for you. As a gift, there will be no charge."

"Thank you, ma'am."

Stan watched Zoë cover the octagon-shaped table with the gold, silken cloth, place the deck of cards in the center, and position the glass ball to her right. He had never visited a psychic, but because he relied heavily on his sixth sense and intuition every day, he was game.

"Please have a seat." Zoë pointed to the ornately carved chair with velvet padded armrests. She sat in the upholstered chair opposite him, smoothed her long skirt, and placed her hands on the tabletop. "How may I help you? Specifically, what is troubling you?"

Stan scratched his head. "Ma'am, that's hard to say, but my mind's been disturbed by feelings that big changes are coming my way. Changes I might not be ready for."

She leaned in and her gold earrings swayed with the movement. "Please call me Zoë. I see an image of an old woman when you say 'ma'am.' Let's begin by holding hands."

Stan offered his large hands palms up and watched Zoë wrap her smaller hands around them as best she could. She closed her eyes and remained silent for a moment.

"You radiate warmth, even on such a day as this. I see you have worked hard and have helped many people along your life's journey; however, the path hasn't been an easy one."

Zoë raised her head and opened her eyes long enough for Stan to see tears glistening at the edges of her eyelids. He had the feeling she could see deep into his soul.

She blinked quickly and whisked away the hint of tears. She concentrated on his hands. "There are elements of pain, loss, and regrets lingering and taking hold of you like a slow-growing cancer." She gently rubbed his palms. "You have a long life line, and I see an opportunity for a second chance at happiness."

"Maybe that's the change I feel coming," Stan said with a catch in his throat.

"Perhaps." Zoë turned his hands over and looked at his knuckles. "These hands have been used for aggression, not fist fighting, though. You have held a gun or a rifle. But not for hunting."

Stan nodded. "I was a Marine, then in law enforcement, now I'm a detective."

"I see." She ran her forefinger over his wrist. "You have broken your right arm several times."

Stan nodded. "One of the hazards of the profession."

Zoë released his hands and wiped her brow with a silk handkerchief she pulled from her skirt pocket. "I am opposed to violence of any kind, but I believe you only use it as a last resort."

Stan didn't reply.

"At this point I'd ask you to shuffle and cut the cards so I can see what they reveal. However, I'm getting a headache, which would prevent me from giving you a proper reading."

"May I come back?"

Zoë thought for a moment. "Tomorrow, at 4 p.m."

"Yes. Until then."

Stan returned to his car. He didn't put on his hat or gloves and ignored the bone-chilling cold. He gripped the steering wheel and tried to digest the possibility Zoë and he had felt an attraction, one beyond that of spiritual advisor and client.

CHAPTER 29
Missing Kittens
and the Man in the Moon

"HERE, WISHY. COME OUT, HOPIN'." Diana crawled on the floor and patted as far under the bed as she could reach. She and Cassie had looked in the closets, behind furniture, and under the bed covers in both of their bedrooms. She stood and put her hands on her hips. "Where the heck are they?"

Cassie shrugged. "Their food doesn't look like it's been touched and the litter box is clean. It's like they weren't even here."

"Maybe they snuck out to explore or are just hiding," Kevin said.

Cassie made a swiping motion with her hand. "No way. Someone must have let them out on purpose. They're used to staying in our rooms. They're still babies." She frowned. "I wonder if Reggie had anything to do with it."

"Who's Reggie?" Kevin asked.

"He's Henry's teenage nephew who's lived here for a few weeks. He helped us move in. But he isn't very friendly. Kind of moody," Diana said.

"Moody? I think he'd do anything to get us to leave. And ..." Cassie seemed to pause for dramatic effect.

"Yeah?" Kevin prompted.

"He might have had something to do with the garage burning down, so we couldn't move in."

"Cass, what a mean thing to say," Diana said.

"Wait. Back up. I saw the burned-out mess when we drove up. Did I hear you right? You were going to live in the garage?" He pointed his thumb toward the window.

"We were ready to move into the two-bedroom apartment *above* the garage, but the night before we moved it went up in a big ball of fire." Cassie waved her arms in a circle for emphasis.

Kevin digested the information for a moment. He cocked his head and squinted. "Has the fire department determined how it started?"

"Not yet. It happened just before Thanksgiving," Diana said.

"Under those circumstances, I don't understand why you agreed to move into the main house without asking more questions. Maybe the fire was a warning by someone who doesn't want anyone snooping around the property."

"Kev. Thank you. I've been trying to tell Diana that all along," Cassie said.

Diana shook her head. "You're reading too much into it. All the buildings are old. It was probably a wiring problem." Before they could counter her comment, she said, "I think that mystery can wait for now. How about we divide up and look for Wishin' and Hopin'?"

Cassie seemed relieved to focus on Wishin' and Hopin'. "Kevin, let's hunt for the kitties. Diana, could you ask Henry if he's seen them and maybe even talk to creepy Reggie?"

"I'll talk to Henry, Reggie, and Miss W, too," Diana said.

An hour later, they sat around the servants' kitchen table. Rose's handwritten note indicated she was at her sister's and would be back between four-thirty and five to prepare dinner. It was almost five. Cassie slumped in her chair. "I think Reggie kidnapped them and dumped them in the woods. The fire didn't discourage us, so he wanted to scare us another way." She leaned forward. "Diana, what did you find out from Henry and Miss W?"

"I told Henry about the missing kittens and he promised to look for them. I asked about Reggie and he told me he's an honor student and has never had a minute of trouble in school. He acted surprised that we'd think Reggie would harm Wishin' and Hopin'. Maybe he's not a monster, just a spoiled kid with an attitude. He isn't here or I would have grilled him."

"What about Miss Winchester, does she have any explanation for everything that's been going on?" Kevin asked.

"You haven't met her." Diana rotated her forefinger around her ear. "She's a little ditzy. She reminded me we weren't supposed to let the kitties out to roam the house." Diana sighed in frustration. "I told her we made sure they were safe in my room with plenty of food and water while we were gone."

"So what did Miss W say about them being missing?" Cassie asked.

"She called us careless girls and warned me if any of her treasures get broken, we have to pay for them."

Cassie blew up. "Diana, we can't stay here any longer. She's a nut job."

Kevin nodded. "I agree. You should move out tonight."

"I can't think straight. Mom's texted me twice asking when we're coming home for dinner."

Kevin stood. "It's too late to do anything tonight. Ready to go?" he asked Cassie.

Cassie let him help her with her coat; afterwards she turned and gazed into his eyes. "Thanks, Kevin."

"Wait, I have to leave a note for Rose and tell her we won't be having dinner with her and Henry." Diana grabbed some notepaper from the desk and scrawled a message. "There, I'm ready. Let's get out of here."

* * *

After dinner, Kevin tried to get Diana alone so they could talk. "Di, we have to iron out our differences. I'm not going home not knowing about us, one way or another."

"I know, but my head is pounding. I need to get to bed." She touched her forehead and stepped back. "We'll talk tomorrow."

"Fine." Kevin decided he needed something to eat. On his way to the kitchen, he bumped into Cassie. "Great minds think alike. Looking for dessert?" he asked.

She held out a half-full pumpkin pie tin. "I can't resist Mrs. Williams' delicious pie. Want a piece?"

"You read my mind. Let's add coffee and sit on the patio. It's more private."

Cassie looked surprised. "Sure. Can you pour the coffee and I'll cut the pie?"

"Be happy to." Kevin grabbed two mugs from the counter.

Cassie peeked around the door to get Emily's attention. "Mrs. Williams, may we excuse ourselves and have our second dessert outside?"

Emily joined them in the kitchen. "Certainly, let me get you a tray."

Kevin and Cassie donned their coats and scarves and sat on the patio. Cassie blew over her mug of coffee and watched the steam dissipate in the cold air. She looked up at the clear night sky and heaved a sigh. "I don't understand why Diana doesn't agree suspicious stuff is going on at Bella Estate."

Kevin sipped his coffee before he responded, "If something's going on, she might not see it because she's a trusting person and makes allowances for people's shortcomings. I'll bet she thinks the garage fire and the kitties' disappearance are coincidences."

He set the cup on the table, tipped his chair back on two legs, and propped his feet on an empty chair. "Diana supported me during my panic attacks, depression, and mood swings. She stayed positive and helped me through my darkest days."

"Then why are you having problems?" Cassie paused. "Are you breaking up?"

Kevin put his feet on the ground and let the chair down with a *thud*. "I don't think she sees it as breaking up, more like taking a break." He leaned forward. "When I came along, she was barely seventeen and had a lot going on in her life. She'd just been told Glenn wasn't her birth father. Then, later that year, Roberta acted even meaner and swung the final blow when she admitted she had kidnapped Diana from the hospital nursery. I know how hard it was for her to hear. I was in the room when it happened.

"Diana and I were separated by two thousand miles." He shrugged. "I guess texts and phone calls couldn't keep the love fires burning." He smiled his trademark crooked grin. "But why am I telling you this? You're her best friend. You know the whole story."

"I'm asking because I thought men fought for their women. They did in caveman days."

"You're comparing me to a caveman?" He felt a surge of adrenaline and smiled.

Cassie wrinkled her nose. "If the shoe fits. Want to take a walk after we finish our pie and coffee?"

"Sure. It's cold, but there's a full moon. Great atmosphere tonight."

They walked four blocks to the city park. Cassie made a bee-line to the swings and sat in one of the larger ones.

"Want a push?" Kevin asked. She nodded and he took hold of the sides of the swing and gave her a gentle shove.

Cassie pumped her legs to go higher and called over her shoulder, "I remember when Diana and I would compete to see who could swing the highest. Then we'd dare each other to jump out." She leaned back on the upswing to gain altitude. "We never broke a bone no matter how high we went or how hard we fell."

"Were you tomboys?" Kevin's head moved like a metronome as he watched her swing.

Cassie dragged the toe of her boot to slow and came to a stop. "Sort of, but we played dolls, took baton lessons, read tons of books in the summer, and were on the same softball team. We were in Blue Birds and Camp Fire Girls together."

Kevin sat in the next swing and twirled it right and left. "Sounds like you had a great childhood. I didn't join clubs, but I played baseball and football, later I took up soccer."

"You look like an athlete." Cassie blushed. "I mean …"

He flexed his arm and jutted his chin. "You can't see them now, but I have a few muscles left. Want to see who can swing the highest?"

"You're on." Cassie dug her foot into the bark dust, leaned back, and pumped her legs up and down.

Before long, they swung in sync for a few minutes; Kevin was quiet and Cassie seemed to be in her own world.

"I'm freezing. I'm stirring up a major wind chill," Cassie said.

"I agree. How about we get a little exercise and warm up?" They climbed the jungle gym and took turns on the slide.

"I haven't done that since I was ten. I'm not cold anymore." Cassie laughed.

"Reminds me of recess in grade school." He paused a beat. "Ready to head back?" Cassie nodded. "I'd like to hold your hand on the walk back, just in case you feel cold again."

"Okay."

Kevin took Cassie's hand and they walked slowly back to the house with the Man in the Moon smiling down.

CHAPTER 30
Sweet Goodbye

"KEVIN, I HOPE YOU UNDERSTAND where I'm coming from," Diana said the next day after lunch.

"I think I know what you're going to say, Di. I'm not an idiot." He shifted on the kitchen chair.

"So much has happened since we met the summer I turned seventeen. I'm not the same person, you've changed, too. We should take a break, start fresh. It's for the best." She played with the fringe on the placemat and avoided his eyes.

"I'm trying to understand. When I was wounded and recovering, you were the strong one. I came to rely on you too much." He looked at his hands and linked his fingers together into one tight fist. "My mother had a rough time with my injury and memory problems. She had to get professional help to deal with the stress."

Diana felt tears running down her cheeks and didn't bother to wipe them away. She tried to divert her attention from her emotions and stabbed at the leftover pie with her fork, but ended up pushing the plate away. *I many never eat pumpkin pie again. It'll remind me of today.*

Kevin touched her hand and gave it a squeeze. "Enough serious talk for now. Do you want me to go with you and Cassie to Bella Estate and look for the kittens one more time?"

"No, let's go, just you and me."

"Okay. I'll get our coats," Kevin said.

"I'll tell Mom we'll be gone for a while. She'll be planning dinner in a couple of hours."

They drove Buffy Bug to Miss W's and told Henry what they were planning. "I surely hope you find your cats soon," he said, "I will keep my eyes open, too."

"Thank you, Henry. They must be scared and hungry. I've been so worried," Diana said.

Kevin and Diana called out for the kitties as they searched the debris in the burned-out garage, the bushes around the main house, and ventured a short distance into the woods. They returned to the kitchen to warm up and relay the sad news to Rose and Henry.

"Here, miss, have some hot coffee; you're frozen half through." Rose clucked over the young people as she poured them coffee.

"Thank you. I am cold." Diana rubbed her hands together and put them around the hot mug Rose set in front of her.

Kevin nodded as he accepted a mug into which he poured a generous amount of cream. "I wish we could have found them. It's a big, bad world out there."

"Mmm, Henry and I promise to look for them every day. I'm partial to cats and until I moved here, I had at least one. Growing up on my daddy's farm, we had so many cats, we couldn't name them all. But Madam doesn't take to house pets. I'm surprised she let your two move in," Rose said.

Henry brought a plate of cookies to the table, pulled up a chair, and took a sip of coffee that Rose had poured for him. "Madam isn't always consistent. She has been acting peculiar lately. I'm worried about her mental state." He looked at Diana. "Don't fret, miss. They will show up. I know it. Rose and I were wondering when you and Miss Cassie are returning."

Diana was tempted to blurt out how Cassie felt about Bella Estate, but didn't want to appear rude. "We're enjoying the Thanksgiving break with family and Kevin, so I'm not sure, but it will be a few more days."

Henry nodded. "I understand, miss. Keep me up to date and we will have your favorite cookies and soda pop on hand."

Diana and Kevin stayed for another hour and said their goodbyes after Emily texted Diana. "We have to go. Mom has dinner in the oven. Cassie and I will be back in a few days and stay at least through December."

"Just through December? I will surely miss you two. It's been a blessing to have young voices ringing through the house," Rose said. Henry nodded.

"Thanks for everything. Say goodbye to Miss W and tell her we'll be back soon."

"We will." Henry stood and walked them to the back door. He tipped his hat.

Diana and Kevin stood on the back porch for a few minutes and scanned the yard one more time for the kittens. "Aren't Rose and Henry the cutest couple?" Diana said.

"They are," Kevin agreed. He put his arm around Diana as they walked to the car. Once inside, Kevin put the key in the ignition, but didn't start the engine.

"Is something wrong?" Diana asked.

"My head tells me it's over, but my heart tells me we might have a future." He looked straight ahead and turned the key.

Diana heard the distinctive whir of the Volkswagen engine; and as she observed Kevin's profile, her thoughts traveled to the first time they sat in Buffy Bug. She and Glenn had spent several hours negotiating with a salesman to purchase her first car. Kevin had gone along for support. Diana remembered how she felt when she turned the key and started the engine of her very first car. She had seen Kevin's reaction. He had a serious expression and was looking straight ahead, just like tonight.

Before Kevin backed the car out of the driveway, Diana put her hand on the steering wheel. "Remember when I bought Buffy?"

"Sure do."

"Do you remember what you said?"

"I wanted you to buy the Volvo because I thought it would be safer."

"That was sweet. I think that's when I fell in love with you." The last three words caught in Diana's throat.

Kevin turned to look at Diana. "I still love you."

"I know." Diana looked at him for a second and then turned her head away. She was tempted to tell him the lie he wanted to hear.

"But that was a long time ago." He paused. "And we're not the same people."

"No, we're not." Diana's resolve returned. "I can't live the life someone else wants me to live. I did that for too many years under Roberta's roof."

"I understand." He touched her left hand and gave it a gentle squeeze. "Everything's going to be okay."

Diana smiled and looked at Kevin. "We will be *more* than okay."

CHAPTER 31
What Do You Want the Most?

CASSIE AND KEVIN SAT across from each other in Portland International Airport's Starbucks while Diana browsed through stores along the concourse. "I hate to see you go, Kevin," Cassie said.

"I wish I didn't have to leave today, but I've already missed two classes."

Cassie took a sip of coffee and gathered her thoughts. "Cooking school doesn't start until January, so it's going to be a long month with not much to do, except worry." She paused. "And putting up with living at crazy Miss W's."

Cassie fumbled for a tissue in her coat pocket, wiped her eyes, and blew her nose more loudly than she meant to. "How ladylike of me." She looked up. "I'm upset about the kittens and Miss Winchester and the whole mess, but ..."

"But what?" Kevin cocked his head.

"The other night you said calling and texting didn't help you and Diana stay together. You two finally had that talk, didn't you?"

Kevin's tone sounded serious. "We did. She and I spent the afternoon together the day after our park date." He sighed. "She wants to move on and as hard as it sounds, I think she's right. Too many things got in our way." He leaned back and hesitated before continuing. "I'm thinking of transferring out at the end of spring semester."

"To Oregon?"

He nodded and gave her his lopsided grin. "I think it's time for a change; it's time to see a new part of the country, to make new friends."

"Really?" Cassie's heart raced with the thought of Kevin living so close.

"We'll talk more later. I've still got to research colleges, programs, and financial aid. Now, let me see your beautiful smile before I leave."

Cassie pushed a stray curl behind her left ear and smiled. She felt embarrassed and overjoyed simultaneously.

Kevin frowned. "I don't like the idea of you two living out there with Reggie and Miss W, the loon. Her tea leaves and Ouija board readings sound weird."

"We're paid up through next month and Miss W won't refund our money. Diana and I talked about it last night and decided to look for an apartment in town and move after the first of the year. Fingers crossed."

Kevin looked at his watch. "I should get in line."

Cassie stopped before they merged into the crowded concourse. "Let me text Diana. She wants to say goodbye."

"Sure."

In less than five minutes, Diana joined them. They stayed with Kevin as the queue edged closer to the security guard.

"See y'all over spring break when I come back to tour colleges," Kevin said.

Diana's eyebrows shot up.

Kevin smiled. "It's been an interesting Thanksgiving for sure." He set his backpack down and took off his shoes to ready himself for the security gauntlet. "Don't you love airports?"

"I like parks better," Cassie said.

"Me, too."

Diana looked from Kevin to Cassie and appeared to put the puzzle pieces together.

The girls waved until he disappeared into the crowd. When Cassie turned toward Diana, she noticed Diana looking at her in a strange way.

"So, Kevin might be moving to Oregon? You seem pretty excited," Diana said.

"Yeah." Cassie sighed. "I can't help myself. I like him."

"I'm happy for you. Maybe it will work out."

"I hope so." Cassie's heart raced at the thought. "It feels right. Just like his name, Kevin Wright. Maybe I found Mr. Right."

"Witty girl." Diana sounded wistful. "I thought I was going to be Diana Wright. Do you remember how I've always talked about being a writer?" Cassie nodded. "My title will just be spelled differently: Diana Julia Louise Williams, Writer."

"Oh, bad pun. But I love the idea of changing your name back to the one your parents gave you. Keeping Diana made sense, though. How about a cinnamon roll and coffee? My treat," Cassie asked.

"Something with chocolate, please. Chocolate always makes me feel better."

* * *

Stan was pleased he could have another reading with Zoë before he left town. He chuckled to himself when he realized he scheduled the session to get to know Zoë rather than have her look into his future. He watched Zoë as she shuffled the tarot cards, spread them out, and interpreted their meaning. Stan wasn't able to concentrate on what she was saying, instead, he daydreamed about asking her on a date. *She's an intelligent, sensitive, and intuitive woman. I doubt she really needs her cards to help people.*

After Zoë concluded their session, Stan asked, "I'd like to take you to dinner tonight if you're available."

She widened her eyes for a second. "My, yes. I don't go out often. It's too depressing to sit at a table by myself."

Stan nodded. "Tell me about it. Any suggestions? I'm not familiar with Boise's hot spots."

"If you like steak, Chandlers Steakhouse is very good. It has a gluten free menu which I prefer. But it's spendy." She tapped the side of her head. "There's Edge Brewing Company and Luciano's."

Stan chuckled. "For not going out much, you know the best restaurants."

"One has to be ready when opportunity knocks." She gathered her cards, placed them in a black, silk handkerchief, and put them in her skirt pocket. Before she got up, Stan tenderly placed his hand over hers.

"I really appreciate what you've done for me. This is the first time I've had a spiritual reading. Been a might skeptical, but I believe you have the Gift."

Zoë appeared to blush. "You're too kind. Not everyone is generous with compliments. Sometimes people demand their money back if I caution them or see things contrary to what they want to hear."

"I take whatever life has to offer, good and bad."

Zoë didn't move her hand away. "You are strong when it counts."

Stan lifted his arm and glanced at his watch. "It's 5:30. If you're willing, we could leave soon. Should I make a reservation?"

"I don't think we'll need to. Just let me tidy up and I'll be with you in say, twenty minutes." She rose with a flourish, her skirt swishing around her legs, and went upstairs.

"I'll wait right here." Stan leaned back and his smile came from his core. He hadn't felt this happy in many years.

* * *

Roberta received a phone call from her lawyer a few days before New Year's Eve. "Berta, I've submitted the Request for Summary Judgment to the court and hope to hear about the scheduling by the middle of February, or early March at the latest."

"Let's hope for good news, too." She paused. "What would you call *good news*?" Roberta lit a tabooed cigarette and hoped Zoë wouldn't notice the smell.

"It would be having the judge order mental evaluations, decide you aren't competent to stand trial, and then commit you to a psychiatric facility. There you would undergo extensive psychological evaluation, subsequent treatment, and confinement for a specified period of time."

"How long do you think the sentence will be? A couple of years?"

Roberta heard a belly laugh from Charles. "Try a minimum of five, maybe longer. The court frowns on kidnapping. How many times have I told you that?"

Roberta crashed on the bed and dropped her cigarette on the rug. "Holy Mother of God. Five years?" She noticed the smell of burning carpet a few seconds later. She stomped on the glowing butt, then picked it up, and threw it in the toilet. Still holding the phone, Roberta stared in the mirror and hated what she saw. Her finger pulsed with pain from the smoldering cigarette, so she ran cold water over it.

Charles continued, "Roberta, karma catches up with us one way or another. Consider it one way the universe equals things out."

"Screw equality. I want mercy. Get me out of this mess."

"We have to wait for this to play out." Roberta heard him cut away for a second. "I have another call I need to take."

"*Fine*. Get back to your rich clients. The ones who'll be celebrating with champagne and caviar when you win their cases."

"Talk to you later, Berta."

Roberta slammed the toilet seat down and sat on it with a *thud.* She leaned forward and put her chin in her hand. *What am I going to do for the next two months? I'm tired of thinking about lawyers, lawsuits, and jail.*

* * *

After looking through the newspaper ads for a week, Cassie couldn't wait to call Diana and share her news. "I found the perfect place to live. The only thing is the landlady told us we couldn't move in until the end of January. She says her son has to make a few minor repairs. I'm sure Miss W won't kick us out before then. She'll like the extra month's rent."

"Is it an apartment?" Diana asked.

"It's a duplex and our half has two bedrooms, laundry room, nice kitchen, and a huge living room. Mrs. Chandler, the owner, lives on the other side."

"Hold on a minute, I'm driving. Okay, I'm on speaker. Where is it?"

"Just off S.W. Vermont Street near Gabriel Park."

"I don't know. Isn't that an expensive neighborhood? How did you find it?"

"I was looking in the Nickle Ads and it popped right out. So I called Mrs. Chandler and told her about us, and how we have a tight budget. She wants to meet us; but she sounds interested because she's particular about who lives next door and would prefer to have two young ladies as renters."

"When can we meet with her?"

"5:30 tonight. The good news is she's okay with pets, so we can bring Wishin', Hopin', and Socks rather than leaving them with your parents."

"It still bugs me we'll never know how Wishin' and Hopin' ended up in the awful wood pile outside Miss W's kitchen. They could have been attacked by a raccoon instead of being just confused, hungry, and scared," Diana said.

"We're lucky Henry and Rose found them in time. It was so sad how the babies stayed in our rooms afterwards and wouldn't even poke their noses into the hallway."

"Yes, but that way they couldn't get us into trouble either." Diana sighed. "I thought it was going to be a great adventure, but I won't miss Bella Estate, at all. Except I'd like to see Henry and Rose again. Miss W couldn't have cared less about the kitties, and Reggie, forget him," Diana said.

"He's a useless, spoiled brat." Cassie sighed. "I think I made a good impression with Mrs. Chandler even though it was over the phone."

"I'm sure you did. I'll be home in a few."

That evening the girls drove to the duplex and met with Mrs. Chandler. From the get-go, Cassie knew it was meant to be and she couldn't quit smiling through the whole interview.

"Cassie, Diana, I couldn't be happier that we'll be neighbors. My son checks in with me every night on his way home from work, and he's very fussy about who lives next door." Mrs. C's cocker spaniel, Blondie, sniffed Cassie's shoe and wagged her tail.

"I can see my dog likes you and she's used to cats so everyone should get along just fine. My son has to make a few repairs in the kitchen and bathroom or you could move in sooner."

"That's okay. It'll work out," Cassie said.

"I'll let you and Blondie get acquainted while I get your house keys. You may come over and measure the rooms for your furniture. I just ask you to call first."

Cassie nodded vigorously. When Mrs. Chandler left the room, Cassie poked Diana on the arm. "Didn't I tell you this would be perfect?"

"I'm glad she didn't talk about séances, tea parties, and magical tea leaves. I was dumb to think Miss W was sane." Diana looked around the living room. "Mrs. C has good taste, too."

Cassie nodded. "This feels normal, not like Miss W's spook house." Cassie leaned back and let out a sigh. "The only drawback is our half isn't furnished, except for appliances."

"Mom has some furniture in the attic, but we'll need dishes and lamps, and such."

"That's what garage sales are for." Cassie leaned over and petted Blondie's head. "Good girl. You'll love our kitties."

Mrs. Chandler returned and handed an envelope to Cassie. "As I said, feel free to come over and get familiar with your apartment. I'll let my son know. He will stop by after you're settled and introduce himself."

"Thank you, Mrs. Chandler. This is an answer to our prayers," Diana said.

"Mine, too, dear, mine too. I won't interfere with your lives, but if you'd like to drop by for tea, you're most welcome. Every afternoon at four, sharp."

Cassie and Diana exchanged looks and stood in tandem. "Thank you, Mrs. Chandler, we'll give you the exact date we can move; but I think it will be closer to the end of January," Diana said.

When the girls got outside, they broke out in laughter. "What is it with old ladies and tea?" Cassie asked.

"Maybe it's a generation thing. At least this time, we'll be prepared for anything strange." Diana smiled. "Although, she *seems* normal."

CHAPTER 32
Roots

JOHN BERGAN CONFESSED his part in Kevin Wright's parentage to his wife and was surprised and relieved she didn't demand an immediate divorce. Their marriage had been rocky for more than two years, but ironically John's indiscretion propelled them to counseling and after several weeks, he could see a marked improvement in their relationship.

However, John had one more hurdle. He wanted to tell Kevin but was unsure of how to broach the subject. He brought it up with his law partner after one of their routine Monday morning meetings.

"Glenn, I haven't spoken to Kevin about me being his father. Any suggestions as to how to break the news?"

"It isn't something you chat about over coffee in Starbucks. I'd pick a private place." He paused a beat and said, "Maybe your marriage counselor would have some ideas."

John leaned back in his chair. "Good idea. She could very well have a few suggestions. Carmella, our counselor, knows everything."

After a call to their counselor, John arranged a meeting with Kevin on the pretext of discussing Calvin's part in Kevin's kidnapping, which was partly true.

* * *

The men met in the lobby of Hotel Arista in Naperville a week later. "Hello, sir." Kevin extended his hand to John in greeting.

"Good to see you, Kevin."

Kevin felt a prickling sensation on the back of his neck, which he refrained from scratching. He shifted his weight from one foot to the other.

"I reserved a table upstairs right outside the bar where lunch will be delivered in an hour or so."

"Okay." Kevin shoved his hands into his coat pockets and followed John to the elevator. He tried unsuccessfully to calm his stomach.

They rode to the second floor in silence. Kevin stared at the door as if it would magically open and alleviate the tension. When the elevator door split, John led the way to a table outside the lounge and overlooking the lobby. "We can talk here in private. The bar doesn't open till four."

Kevin disliked hotels. He was having a flashback to the day he, Diana, and Big Stan stood in the hallway outside Roberta's hotel room in Astoria, Oregon when they went to question her about Diana's past. Roberta's response was to pull a gun on Big Stan, which was a huge mistake on her part. Kevin started to sweat profusely and discovered he couldn't move a muscle. The elevator doors began to close.

John turned at the sound and stepped over to put his hand in front of the partially closed door. "Is something wrong?" he asked.

"I, uh, no." Kevin forced his legs to move as he followed John down the hall, all the while feeling something big was about to come down.

They sat at a two-table. Kevin looked downstairs through the glass partition and felt nauseated when a wave of vertigo washed over him.

"I'll make this as uncomplicated as possible." John wiped his brow and appeared to struggle with words. "We have a great deal in common and I needed a quiet place to talk over a few things. This is better than the café downstairs."

Kevin forced himself to keep up with John's train of thought. "Mr. Bergan, is this about Calvin?"

"In part. This will take a few minutes. Then we can order lunch, if you want to stay, that is."

"If I look stressed …" Kevin twisted in his swivel chair to get comfortable, but found it didn't help. "It's because I still suffer from PTSD. It's an annoying side effect from my injuries and amnesia."

John nodded. "I'm well aware of your condition and I'm sorry to say I bear some responsibility."

Kevin was puzzled. "I don't understand."

"I have a lot to share." John leaned forward, clasped his hands together, and looked at them for a few seconds.

John told Kevin the circumstances of how he had met his birth mother, and how she became pregnant after their one night together. Kevin grimaced inwardly and outwardly when he realized he was the product of a brief, very brief affair.

"Are you okay?" John asked when he saw Kevin's reaction.

"It's a shock to hear how I was conceived." He paused. "I guess I should be grateful she didn't have an abortion."

It was John's turn to wince. Kevin felt a shockwave go through his body. "You asked her to have an abortion, didn't you?"

"She wanted to keep you. But she also wanted me to marry her. I told her that was impossible. There was no way I could tell my wife about the pregnancy." John squirmed in his chair. "A year or so later, I received a letter from her telling me you had been adopted privately."

"I guess you paid her off," Kevin said.

"I made sure she had good medical care, if that's what you mean."

Kevin felt determined to find out as much as he could. "What did you do when you found out I was adopted?"

John smiled grimly. "I discovered your adoptive parents were from Naperville. I think she deliberately chose a couple who lived in the same town as me."

"Revenge?" Kevin asked.

"I'd rather think of it as making it easier for me to see you."

Kevin struggled to keep up with John's revelations. He had known about his adoption and sometimes wondered who his birth parents were. However, it was a big dose of reality to discover his father was Glenn's law partner and that they had always lived in the same city. He was amazed to discover he had known his half-brother ever since elementary school.

John asked, "How do you feel about this, son?"

Kevin felt a surge of anger when John called him 'son.' His mouth felt dry and he tried to swallow. "Do you know what happened to my birth mother?"

John slowly shook his head. "We lost touch. I have no idea."

"Does Glenn know about you and me?"

"Not until recently. In fact, I might never have told him except for Calvin's kidnapping."

Kevin looked at John with a laser beam stare before he asked, "What happened exactly? Did the police ever find the thugs? Were they the same guys who kidnapped me? Did they identify the burned body found in the Corvette?"

John put his hands up as if in surrender. "Whoa. That's a lot to go over. Do you want me to discuss all this now?"

Kevin shrugged. "Might as well. I don't know when we'll see each other again."

John placed his palms on his knees, took a deep breath, and began, "It was in the papers, but you could have missed the article. Calvin escaped and was able to tell the authorities where he had been held. They made a raid within hours, rounded up the group, and they sang like magpies. Authorities apprehended the head guy a few days later. Turns out, the burned body was one of their own. They stole the Corvette when they grabbed Calvin." He paused. "The corpse was working deals on the side and pocketing money. But when he turned on a couple of his friends, they told the boss and that's when they found revenge."

"Why did they kidnap me and Calvin?" Kevin interrupted.

"You two look a lot alike. They were after Calvin. He was dealing marijuana and owed them a few thousand. He dodged them for a while, but couldn't fly under their radar forever. They demanded payoff for monies owed; and unfortunately, there was a mix-up, which led to your beating and abduction last year."

Kevin took a sip of water and looked over the glass wall into the lobby. When he didn't respond, John said, "I know this is a lot to absorb in one sitting." He rubbed his hands together as if to warm them.

Kevin looked at John for thirty or more seconds before he said, "It'll take me a while to think everything through." He felt his hands grow clammy and wiped them on his jeans. "As for my adoptive parents, they didn't tell me anything about my birth mother or birth father. Maybe they didn't know their identities. When I was older, I told them I didn't care. But …" He shook his head to dismiss the memories.

"When the police on both sides of the border failed to find me after the kidnapping last year, my parents hired Glenn. His detectives found me in Canada where I was recovering from amnesia and other injuries. I couldn't ask for a better family. They've given me everything. From day one."

John leaned forward a few inches, which sparked Kevin's defense mechanism. Kevin pulled back, stood, and lost his composure. He turned away and quietly cried for a couple of minutes before he gathered his thoughts.

"I'll leave you alone for a while and order lunch. Do you want something?"

"A sandwich would be great. Doesn't matter what kind." Kevin didn't have an appetite, but he wanted John out of his sight, if even for a few minutes.

John stood and headed to the elevator. Kevin watched him walk away. He took three deep breaths to clear his head and walked to the end of the hall. As he looked out the window to the courtyard below he thought, *How can I tell Mom and Dad I know who my birth father is? What will they think, what will they do?*

A few minutes later, Kevin heard the elevator. He returned to the table and waited for John.

"Lunch will be up in fifteen minutes."

Over lunch Kevin picked at his food. Rather than eating, he asked John more questions.

"Did you watch me while I was growing up?" Kevin asked.

"When I heard a Naperville couple had adopted you, I kept my eye out. I was able to guess your identity after you and Calvin started school. Your mutual looks and gestures were a giveaway." John paused. "I kept track of you from then on."

Kevin was surprised at this revelation. "So, were you going to keep this a deep, dark secret?" He felt more pain seeping in and found it difficult to control his rising anger.

John nodded. "Absolutely. I didn't want to upset you or your adoptive parents. What would I have gained by coming forward?"

Kevin kept silent.

"But with all that's happened I had to say something. You and Calvin were put in great danger and could have been killed. The truth took precedent over my embarrassment." He rubbed his forehead. "I couldn't play the charade any longer."

"I will never call you *Dad*." Kevin's tone took on a harsh edge.

John looked hurt, but said, "I didn't think you would, or should. You have parents who loved and raised you, and sacrificed so much. I did none of those things."

Kevin stood. "Thank you for lunch, and for the truth. It explains a lot."

"I suspect you need time, but I hope you will call me." John walked Kevin to the elevator where they shook hands and parted.

* * *

Kevin made it to the car and sat motionless, barely breathing, and held the steering wheel for support. *I need to talk to someone.* The obvious choice was the one woman who would understand. He tossed the keys on the passenger seat and reached for his phone.

"Diana, do you have a few minutes to talk?"

"I do." She paused. "You sound funny. Is anything wrong?"

Kevin adjusted the driver's seat to be more comfortable and told his story. He appreciated Diana's willingness to hear him out without interruption.

"Kevin, I sympathize and understand what a blow this is for you. My world turned upside down when Roberta told me Glenn wasn't my father. When she admitted she kidnapped me from the hospital, it was horrible. But the truth was freeing."

"My truth is too raw right now." He rubbed his temple trying to ease his pounding headache. "I hope to feel different in a few days."

"You will. I suggest you talk to Cassie. She'll understand."

Kevin nodded to himself. "I know it's over between us, but I wanted you to know first. Please don't say anything. I have to process this before I talk to Cassie or my parents." He forced a laugh. "Good fodder for my therapist."

"Your news is safe with me. Take care, Kev. I hope we'll stay friends."

"Always. Thanks for listening. I knew you'd understand." He hung up, wiped his damp eyes, and grabbed his car keys.

CHAPTER 33
Moving On

THE GIRLS MOVED into Mrs. Chandler's duplex on February 1; however, the move was not without drama on Miss Winchester's part. "Girls, I am so disappointed. I thought we made a marvelous team, except for your mischievous kittens." She invited them to High Tea in hopes of convincing them to stay; but the gesture fell flat when they refused due to a prior engagement.

Diana couldn't wait to leave Bella Estate for good and kept edging toward the front door.

"I'm sorry, Miss Winchester, but we found the long commute difficult. We do appreciate your generosity in letting us stay in the main house for two months, though. It must have been an inconvenience. We will miss Rose and Henry, too. Please let them know in case they don't return from grocery shopping in time."

"I will not speak to the servants on your behalf." Miss W made it clear by her tone and facial expressions she was *not pleased*. "And I hope you weren't expecting your cleaning deposit returned or a reference for future landlords."

"I guess not," Diana said as she shook in anger; however, she managed to offer her hand in goodbye. Miss Winchester appeared reluctant, but accepted Diana's gesture.

"You have certainly made me re-think whom I choose to live under my roof," Miss W said before she turned and left the room. Diana heard the hall door shut a little more firmly than usual.

"Try not to laugh, Cassie. If she hears you, she'll really get mad." Cassie cupped her hand over her mouth, but Diana saw her broad grin underneath.

As they drove away with the last of their possessions stuffed in the backseat of Buffy Bug, Cassie commented, "Hey, at least we're getting out of this arrangement with Miss W alive, not to mention Wishin' and Hopin'."

"True, but I hate to part ways on a bad note." Diana saw the irony in her comment as she reflected on her last conversation with Roberta.

* * *

Diana's brother and father helped them move into the duplex; however, their off-and-on struggle with the bulky pieces turned out to be somewhat comical to watch. "Dad, I can hold up my end of the couch, don't be so bossy," Bryan complained as they struggled while maneuvering the old sectional through the front door.

"I'm not trying to boss you, son. I don't want to damage the couch, the door frame, or either of us."

Diana chuckled to herself as she watched them contort their bodies through the door. "Don't worry about the couch, Dad. As Mom said, it's seen better days."

"So have I," James said. He set his end down when they got to an open spot, and wiped his brow. "I'm glad you aren't moving in July."

By the end of the afternoon, the four called the move a success and enjoyed a late lunch at Fat City Café in Multnomah Village. "I can't get enough of their delicious french fries," James said. He leaned back in his chair and patted his stomach.

"Be careful, Dad, it isn't called Fat City for nothing," Diana said.

"Anytime you need help, give me a call and then we can check out Fat City's dessert menu," James joked.

"I hear their homemade cherry and apple pies are to *die* for," Diana said.

* * *

Their living arrangement at Mrs. Chandler's turned out to be a godsend for all parties. The girls felt safe living in a family oriented neighborhood and had the privacy they didn't have at Diana's or Bella Estate.

Mrs. C gave them a first-year anniversary party on Valentine's Day, complete with tea, ladyfinger sandwiches, fruit, and a wide variety of desserts. "Girls, this year has been such a blessing. My son can't say enough nice things about what good renters you've been. The new paint and shiny waxed floors make the apartment look brand new. And everything is always so neat and tidy." She knew this because Diana and Cassie had invited her over several times.

Diana had her mouth full with a chocolate macaroon cookie, so Cassie jumped in. "We love it here, Mrs. C. It's right on the bus line and close to everything."

"We *are* in an excellent location." Her eyes grew misty. "The only sad part is the passing of my dear, sweet Blondie just before Christmas. I'm afraid years of epilepsy were hard on her heart."

Both girls nodded. "It is sad. I know Wishin', Hopin', and Socks miss her, too," Diana said.

"Ah, well. I'm thinking of getting a rescue dog. I can't handle a puppy at my age."

"What a good idea. If you need help with it, just ask," Cassie added.

"That reminds me. I have some lovely embroidered hankies my late sister sewed. Would you each like one or two?"

Diana glanced at Cassie who first wrinkled her nose, then smiled. "That would be nice, Mrs. Chandler. Maybe we can carry them when we get married," Cassie said.

Diana's eyes opened wide at Cassie's unexpected remark. "Oh, land sakes. What a wonderful thing that would be. And I hope to be there for both of you on your wedding days." Mrs. Chandler pulled out *her* ever-present hanky and brushed away a tear.

Diana and Cassie continued their living arrangement in the duplex for another year during Diana's final year at Portland Community College and Cassie's culinary studies. But when Diana enrolled as a junior at the University of Portland, she couldn't resist the call of campus life.

"Cass, I'd like to find an apartment next to the U. I don't want to feel out of touch by being a commuter."

Cassie leaned back in the leather chair in their favorite Starbucks in southwest Portland. "I knew this day would come." She let out a heavy sigh.

Diana sensed Cassie was close to tears and interjected, "What do you mean?"

Cassie took a gulp of her coffee and shrugged. "With graduation and looking for my first real job as a cook, I was ready for challenges and change. But I really hate the thought of looking for a new roommate."

"New roommate?" Diana was shocked.

"I assume you'll want to room with a university student."

Diana leaned closer. "You couldn't be more wrong. I was hoping you'd think about making the move, too. Remember back when I moved in with you and your mom our senior year of high school?"

Cassie nodded.

"We promised to be like Lucy Ricardo and Ethel Mertz. Friends forever. As long as we both live in Portland, we can't split up." Diana turned serious. "I've been wondering if Mrs. C will be renting her duplex much longer. Have you noticed she seems a little senile?"

Cassie nodded again. "She repeats herself quite a bit and didn't recognize me a couple of times. She kind of reminds me of how you describe Grandma Louise."

"It's all so sad. I wouldn't be surprised if her son moves her to an adult home. And he might even have to sell her house to pay the expenses." Diana felt depressed at the thought of Mrs. Chandler moving into assisted living. She knew firsthand how quickly her grandmother was going downhill and how hard it was for the nursing staff to give consistent individualized care.

* * *

Three months later the girls moved into an apartment building a few blocks from the University and right on a downtown bus line. "Cass, our apartment is going to work out great," Diana said.

Cassie scooched back in her favorite overstuffed chair in Starbucks and tucked her feet up. "All of our furniture fits, the cats have settled in, and the maple trees next to the balcony are the perfect place for them to hang out. I am worried about them harassing the birds, though."

"If the birds are smart, they'll avoid our trees. I hope the cats don't get scared being outside so much. It's all so new for them; and Hopin' hates heights. I see her watching Socks and Wishin' from the balcony all by herself. Poor thing."

"They're doing fine. Now, if we could have a decent *date* once and a while, the weekends wouldn't seem so long." She waved her Danish pastry in the air. "But my Fridays and Saturdays will fill up as soon as I get a full-time job in a hotel or restaurant."

"Umm." Diana nodded as she swallowed the last of her muffin. "The perfect job will come along sooner than you think."

"I sent my application to the Heathman Hotel. Sure hope I hear back soon."

"In the meantime, don't settle for *any* date. I'm holding out for a guy with more than a charming smile and a big ego," Diana mused.

Cassie gazed out the window. "My dream is to hear from Kevin. The last time he called was right after he had that talk with his birth father. That was eons ago."

Diana hoped her friend wouldn't be upset when she said, "He called me a couple of times after he talked with John." Cassie looked surprised. "He said Glenn was helping him work through some legal issues."

"With the kidnapping?"

"That and he was trying to find his birth mother."

"Wow. Did he?"

"I don't know. Glenn never said, and I didn't hear from Kevin again." Diana watched Cassie absorb the news. "Are you okay?"

"So it wasn't me; I guess he didn't call back because he decided to stay in Illinois to work things out with his family." She blinked quickly and wiped her nose with her napkin.

"That sounds reasonable." Diana tried to sound encouraging.

Cassie sniffled, her voice cracked. "I can't believe how selfish I've been. All this time, I thought he was being a jerk. But he had serious problems to work out."

Diana nodded. "He sure did."

"Well, you've handled all the garbage that Roberta threw at you pretty well."

"For the most part, but I've decided to get counseling to work out my anger issues."

Cassie looked surprised again. "You are?"

"I don't want to carry these dark feeling around any longer."

Cassie uncurled her legs and stretched them out. "I hate that you've had to deal with such a selfish person." She leaned forward and lowered her voice. "Today has turned out to be quite a shocker. When I think about how much others have gone through, I realize how fortunate I am having the greatest mom and Glenn as the perfect stepdad."

"Plus you've had me as a best friend since grade school; and now I'm your sister, too," Diana added.

"We're pretty lucky. Us being roommates and friends for so long, it's a miracle we've never had serious disagreements." Cassie smiled.

"Why don't we celebrate? Do you want to splurge and eat out tonight?"

"I sure do. But where?" Cassie asked.

"I've heard the Heathman Hotel's dining room is totally amazing."

CHAPTER 34
Dreams Fulfilled

THE FIRST YEAR TOGETHER in their apartment flew by. Cassie began her job as a sous-chef at the Heathman Hotel, and Diana blossomed after she switched majors to Special Education mid-way through her junior year. She didn't want to delay graduation, so with the help of her adviser she chose her classes carefully.

Diana's life took another positive turn when she met Roger Archibald, a teaching assistant to one of her classes, and accepted his invitation to a Valentine's dance held at the Hilton. He impressed her with an orchid corsage, a limousine ride, and an elaborate dinner at a five-star restaurant.

Diana tried not to fall in love with Roger that evening, but as she danced in his arms, she felt he was the yin to her yang and hoped it was only a matter of time for him to feel the same way.

He must have had the same feelings for Diana; they dated exclusively and saw each other almost every day. However, a few months later, they were at a crossroad. Diana wasn't surprised with his invitation to move into his condo, but she rejected the offer, even though she feared her decision would end their relationship.

"Roger, you know that I love you, but I don't think it's a good idea for us to live together," Diana said.

"Why the heck not?" His trademark good humor seemed to evaporate.

"My folks wouldn't like it. They're traditional."

Roger had parked the car outside Diana's apartment building. He shifted in the driver's seat, leaned closer to Diana, and put his forefinger under her chin. "You're twenty-one and haven't lived with your parents for three plus years. They'll get over it. What other choice to they have?" He kissed her gently on the lips and smiled.

Diana pulled away a few inches. "I guess I'm traditional, too. I'd like to finish college and maybe even get a teaching job before I make a commitment."

"I'm not asking for a *commitment*. Just a more comfortable living arrangement." He winked. "Or are you putting on the pressure?"

Diana was confused. "Pressure?"

"You want to be engaged first. Go the *traditional* route."

"I didn't say anything about getting engaged. You assume too much." Diana felt her face flush with anger. "We've only been dating since February."

"All the more reason to move in. We can get to know each other better."

Diana shook her head. "I don't think it always works that way. Besides, I'm not ready, not yet." She made a move to get out of the car.

Roger touched her arm. "Wait a minute, please."

Diana looked into his eyes, which seemed to say, *Don't be mad.* "I guess I can't be angry at you for trying." She leaned over and brushed his lips with a kiss.

"I thought you would be all for it. I miscalculated. Sorry."

"See you tomorrow?" Diana asked.

"Sure thing. Pick you up after your three o'clock class." He pulled her in close for a kiss; his lips lingered. When they separated, he murmured, "Sweet dreams."

Diana hopped out and waved as Roger slowly pulled into traffic. She entered the empty apartment. It was apparent Cassie wasn't home from the dinner shift at the hotel. Diana leaned against the door and smiled at the memory of Roger's kiss that still tingled her lips.

Socks ran over and rubbed against Diana's leg. "Hello, sweetie. Have a good day?" She picked up the cat and nestled its soft fur against her cheek. "Always here for me, aren't you?" As if in agreement, Socks meowed and rubbed her nose against Diana's face. Wishin' and Hopin' scampered from the bedroom. "Come on, kids, let's get some ice cream!"

* * *

Diana completed her degree requirements and graduated from the University of Portland in May, as Cassie climbed the ranks in Heathman Hotel's kitchen. Diana applied for and was offered a teaching job in the Portland Public School District, while Cassie was on the move to find a position in a larger city.

"I've grown to love Portland, but I don't see me getting ahead by staying here," Cassie said one afternoon while they lounged in their customary chairs at their favorite Starbucks.

"Now it's my turn to be depressed about losing my roommate. Where do you want to go?" Diana asked.

"Chicago or New York City."

"Wow, you're serious about this aren't you?"

Cassie nodded as she popped the last of her muffin in her mouth. "Sure am," she mumbled.

"You've done so well at the Heathman, it's only a matter of time before you find your dream job." Diana's excitement over her crisp new teaching certificate and job to match evaporated.

"Don't hold your breath. I'm not going to take just any job. Meanwhile, you're going to be my guinea pig. I have a ton of recipes I want to try on you."

Diana brightened. "Let's have a dinner party. Remember the movie *Julie and Julia* where Julie cooked her way through Julia Child's French cookbook and served lobster and fabulous desserts to her friends?"

"Great idea." Cassie looked pensive as she counted on her fingers. "You and Roger, your folks, and Chuck, my partner in crime at the hotel, can come to our first party." She hopped up. "I've got to write some ideas down before I forget."

Diana smiled. She was excited for Cassie, but wasn't looking forward to her moving away. *Change.* Diana hated not the word as much as how insecure it made her feel.

* * *

It was mid-summer, one of the hottest days on record. Cassie returned to their stifling apartment between a split shift at the Heathman and found Diana sitting on the floor in front of their large fan with her shirt raised a bit.

"Hey, girlfriend, cooling down?" Cassie asked as she closed the door and set her purse on the chair.

Diana nodded and held up her glass of lemonade with her free hand as if to make a toast. "I'm trying." She crisscrossed her legs, rose in one fluid motion, and reclined on the couch. "I haven't heard how your job search is going in a long time. I get the feeling it's a deep, dark secret."

"I've narrowed it, or I've been narrowed down to two, both of which are grrrreat!" Cassie responded.

"Where?"

"I don't want to jinx it, so yes, it is a secret for now." Cassie joined Diana on the couch and plopped her sandaled feet on the coffee table. "But I should hear good news or bad soon."

"When you do, I want to be the first to know."

"Don't worry, Di, you're my go-to girl."

By late summer, Cassie still hadn't given Diana an update. But when Diana picked up the mail Monday afternoon and saw two large envelopes for Cassie with intriguing return addresses, she wondered what life changing news was in store.

That evening, Cassie burst into their apartment with a flushed face and unrestrained excitement. "Guess what!" she said as she tossed two shopping bags on the floor.

"You got a job."

At the sound of Cassie's louder than normal entrance, three cats ran down the hall and skidded to a stop at the front door. Their whiskers twitched in anticipation.

Cassie talked so fast, Diana could hardly keep up. "I got an email at noon from one hotel and an hour later, from the other. I couldn't say anything at work, so I've been busting with the news."

"What did you find out?"

Cassie danced an Irish jig for a few seconds and announced, "I've been invited to interview for the sous-chef position at the Park Hyatt Chicago and … at the Crowne Plaza Times Square. They said paperwork is coming snail mail. Why I don't know."

"You'll know soon. Two envelopes came for you today." Diana pointed to the mail on her grandmother's antique secretary.

"Super." Cassie grabbed one and tore it open.

"What's inside?" Diana asked.

"Brochures, a sample contract, another questionnaire." Cassie tossed the papers on the coffee table.

"I couldn't be happier for you. Which do you prefer?"

Without hesitation, Cassie said, "The Park Hyatt. It would be fab to live closer to Mom and Glenn, but who could refuse New York City?"

"Not me, that's for sure. When are the interviews?"

"The Park Hyatt is in two weeks and the Crowne Plaza a week after that."

"How weird is it that you heard from both on the same day."

Cassie joined Diana on the couch. "Yes and no. Hotels look for new talent a few months before the holidays. That way if some don't work out, there's a backup list. I saw the first email on my lunch break, so I ran to Nordstrom and bought two outfits."

"You didn't waste any time." Diana laughed. "Show me what you bought."

"Will do." Cassie grabbed her packages and headed to the bedroom to change, with the cats at her heels.

CHAPTER 35
The Next Course

CASSIE HAD BEEN AT THE PARK HYATT Chicago for barely a month when Diana called her with news. "Cass, I know it's been a while since we've talked. I couldn't send this in a text. Are you sitting down?"

"Sitting down, I'm in bed." Cassie yawned. "It's 1 a.m., girl."

"Sorry. I forgot. But I couldn't wait to ask you something."

"I'm awake. Shoot."

"Will you be my maid of honor?"

"What? I didn't know you were engaged," Cassie squealed.

"As of last night. While Roger and I were having dinner, he popped the question over dessert. He waited until I had a mouthful of chocolate cake before he took the ring out of his pocket and asked me to marry him."

"It's about time. You've been dating like forever." Cassie giggled. "I remember Roger has a goofy sense of humor. I'm surprised he didn't drop the ring in a glass of champagne or have the waiter slip it into your cake."

"Funny. He's very romantic. After I accepted, he slipped it on my finger and I forgot all about my cake. And you know how much I love dessert."

"Roger was taking a chance. Tough choice: cake, ring, hmm."

Diana laughed. "We set the date for September 20th. Can you schedule it?"

"Not to worry. But that's only four months away. Will you have enough time to get everything done?" Cassie sounded concerned.

"I'll make it happen. I have the names of two wedding planners and three bridal boutiques. Mom wants to help and so do the girls." Diana referred to her twin sisters, Kate and Kerri. "But I'd like your opinion on bridesmaids' dresses."

"You just got the ring and the wedding's half planned. I bet you've chosen your colors and everything."

"You know me. Miss Organized. I've always wanted to have an outdoor September wedding. I'm using burnt orange and cream with silver and black accents. I'll carry white calla lilies and wear a cream-colored silk gown. The bridesmaids will carry orange callas. I hope black doesn't turn people off."

"Not unless you drape black streamers along the aisle or wear a black veil." Cassie chuckled.

"Nooo, black is for the attendants' dresses and the men's suits. It'll be a formal late afternoon wedding."

"Good call. I look thin in black."

"I'll text you with more details. I could use an expert's suggestions for the dinner menu. If you have time, that is. How's it going with your job at the Hyatt?"

"I love it, but the hours are long with no time off on weekends or holidays. Not much of a personal life, but I do see Mom and Glenn quite a bit."

"Your personal life will pick up. Maybe you'll meet someone at the reception. There's a huge dance floor at the Forestry Center and we'll hire a live band."

"Then be sure and invite plenty of single men." Cassie laughed.

"I'm so proud of you. Not many would land a job at a five-star Chicago hotel so early in their career. I'm jealous you're living so close to Glenn and Maggie."

"That's one reason I took the job, plus I really wanted to live in an exciting city with unlimited possibilities."

"I understand. New scenery, fresh start."

"I hate to cut this short, Di, but I'm exhausted. Talk tomorrow?"

"Sure, sorry for calling so late. Bye, Cass."

"Bye. Love to your family, especially Roger."

Diana hung up and curled up on the couch. She remembered how guilty she felt after breaking up with Kevin; after which she wondered if the Love Bug would bite her again. The pain and confusion from Roberta's betrayal and the realization she wasn't ready for a romantic commitment made her doubt her ability to make good decisions.

Diana looked at her solitaire diamond ring set in platinum, kissed the gem, buffed it on her shirt, and held it to the light. It wasn't the largest diamond ever, but it sparkled brilliantly and reflected how she felt on the inside. "Roger, our life together will be wonderful."

CHAPTER 36
Getting from There to Here

THE JOURNEY FROM IDENTIFYING as a victim to victor wasn't an easy road for Diana to travel. It had taken a year of professional counseling during her senior year at the University to resolve negative feelings for Roberta bordering on hatred.

Diana also recognized Roger's deep love had helped her make the transition, too. She could hear his voice echoing in her ear, "Di, don't let Roberta's mistake chart the course of your life. You have to heal and move on."

"I won't see or talk to her, ever," Diana insisted at first.

"You don't have to contact Roberta in order to forgive her," he had said.

"You sound like my counselor."

"It doesn't matter where Roberta is or what she thinks or does. It's what's in your mind and heart that matters."

Diana's father echoed Roger's sentiments. "Sweetheart, your mother and I are moving on with life. So must you."

Zoë wanted to help Diana go the final mile after she told her Roberta had been classified as a model patient. Because she had served half of her five-year confinement in the Oregon State Hospital, she qualified for a supervised leave under special circumstances.

"Diana, she isn't same person you remembered as a child," Zoë insisted.

"Roberta couldn't have changed a lifetime of habits in two years," Diana told her friend.

"Do you want to visit her at the hospital and see for yourself?" Zoë asked.

Diana choked on the thought. "Why would I want to do that? She's always dumped cold water or a pile of crud on me when anything positive came my way."

Zoë looked pensive. "I have no knowledge of your relationship with Roberta, only snippets she's told me along the way. Give it a little more time then, sweetie." She played with the fringe on her shawl.

"She and I have had long talks and she really feels terrible about what she did to you and your parents. I think a visit could set things on the right track. It's not like she has a busy social calendar."

Diana didn't respond.

Zoë shifted gears a bit. "When Stan and I moved to Portland last year, it was more convenient to be Roberta's regular visitor. I also applied to be her advocate."

Diana ignored the Roberta part of the conversation and said, "I was so excited when you and Stan moved to Portland. We'll see you at the wedding, and then we'll have to get together after Roger and I are settled."

Zoë leaned forward. "I can't wait. After my sweet husband retired, we thought living in a larger community would help grow my business." She smiled. "I'm getting close to signing a lease for a tea shop so I can combine selling tea, herbs, and essential oils under one roof."

"How exciting. I wish you great success. Living here may be easier on your joints, too."

"Sweetheart, you remembered I suffer from arthritis."

"Have your herbal supplements and essential oils helped?"

"Yes. I don't know where I'd be without them." Zoë held up her hands and wiggled her fingers. "I couldn't do this a few months ago. Idaho winters are brutal on aging joints."

Diana smiled. "You've always had the most beautiful hands of anyone I've known. Okay, I'll be sending out wedding invitations before too long and I'll need your new address."

"I'll give it to you straight away, and what about Roberta?"

"I don't know."

"I will be looking forward to positive news, my dear;" Zoë said.

However, Emily was not completely on board when Diana mentioned the possibility of inviting Roberta to the wedding. "Even though your dad and I are moving on, it's possible she could ruin the happiest day of your life."

Despite her mother's reluctance to help with the guest list and reception seating, Diana's twin sisters and Cassie made sure all of the plans fell into place. She cringed remembering the tension between her and her mother; Diana wanted to make things right. *Dad and I always end up being the peacemakers in the family.*

Emily was insistent and remained dead-set against having Roberta attend, even after Diana asked her to have an open mind. She had forgiven Roberta for kidnapping her from the hospital nursery and was considering offering an olive branch by inviting her to the wedding. "Maybe Roberta wouldn't want to attend, anyway," Diana had said. She knew all too well it had never been easy to predict Roberta's moods or reactions.

* * *

Diana and Roger met for dinner that night and talked about the possibility of her visiting Roberta in the State hospital. "Zoë thought it was a good idea. What do you think?" she asked.

"You have to decide what feels right for you."

"Big help you are," Diana said.

"Okay, here goes." Roger struck a serious demeanor. "If my mother ..."

"She's not and never has been my mother," Diana interrupted.

"Sorry. If the woman I *thought* was my mother for seventeen years was in a mental hospital and appeared to be making good progress, I'd make one visit. If nothing else, to clear the air, move on, take the high ground." Diana winced at Roger's words. He continued, "You were thinking of inviting her to the wedding. What's the difference?"

"I'd be afraid to see her alone in a sterile hospital setting. Besides, you have no idea what she put me and my parents through."

Roger slowly nodded. "You're right. But don't you want to put this behind you forever?"

"Of course."

"One last face-to-face in a controlled environment might do it. The medical staff won't put you at risk."

"I don't know ..." Diana felt a tension headache coming on. She massaged her forehead with her fingers for a few seconds before she continued, "I haven't seen her in years – ever since our blowup in the hospital when she confessed to kidnapping me from the nursery."

Roger reached across the table and gently took her hand in his. "How dreadful it must have been for you."

Diana felt tears welling up and spilling onto her cheeks. She pulled her hand away and fumbled for a tissue in her purse. After she blew her nose, she said, "Kevin was with me. If I'd been alone, I don't know what would have happened."

"I can't imagine. But, give it some thought. Say the word and I'll drive you down. Then I will be close by to rescue you in case things go south."

"What about my dumb idea of inviting her to the wedding?"

He took Diana's left hand in his and kissed each finger. "Make that decision later. There's no rush."

* * *

Two weeks later, over coffee Diana told Roger she had decided to visit Roberta. "I'm glad, sweetheart. I think it will help you immeasurably." He smiled and sat back in the chair.

"I'm not as optimistic as you. However, I did talk to Dad about it and he agreed."

"What about you mother?"

Diana shook her head. "No way. She's still furious, hurt, stubborn. She doesn't understand where I'm coming from. But, I'll deal with that later."

"Make the appointment and I'll clear the day."

"Thanks. I know you're busy with clients and the big remodel job downtown."

"Mmm, but nothing's more important than you." He half rose, leaned over the café table, and kissed her passionately on the lips.

* * *

Diana and Roger arrived at the Oregon State Hospital facility on an unseasonably cold, rainy day in late June. "Wouldn't you know. The weather couldn't be worse. So depressing. It's been gorgeous the last three weeks. I hope it doesn't do this for our wedding in September," Diana said.

Roger reached over and held Diana's left hand. His thumb brushed the solitaire on her ring finger. "Don't fret, we'll be in and out, and then go to dinner."

Diana didn't respond; instead, she looked out the window. She watched the rain pelt the car and thought about how much she resented all the time and energy Roberta had taken from her life. *How many times has she hurt and disappointed me?* She hiccupped. *This is the last time I'm making the effort.* She clenched and unclenched her right fist.

At the entrance to the facility, Diana watched the armed guard behind the glass barrier check their identification. When she glanced up and saw a cadre of security cameras staring at them, she felt a shiver go down her spine. They had passed through the first layer of security. Inside the main gate, another formidable-looking guard checked their IDs, flipped through his visitors' schedule, gave them the once-over, and waved them through.

Roger parked the car and held Diana's arm at her elbow as they approached the building. At the front door, he pressed a button, which roused an unseen voice that said, "Can I help you?"

Diana said, "Yes, I'm Diana Williams and I have an appointment to visit Roberta Baker."

Two minutes later, they heard a loud buzz and the front door opened. Stepping into the vestibule, her heart skipped a couple of beats when she realized where she was and what was about to happen. The nurse waved her over; Diana approached and pulled out her identification. The nurse scrutinized it and checked her schedule. She handed the ID back and made a call. After hanging up, she simply said, "Wait here for the escort, miss. He stays here." She pointed to Roger.

"This is where I have to leave you, Di," Roger said.

Diana looked around the sterile room. "Here?"

"There's a bench for me to sit on. Don't worry." He kissed her forehead and winked.

She felt tears welling in her eyes. "Hopefully it won't be too awful."

He kissed her nose and mouth. "Stay strong."

Diana heard someone clearing her throat; she looked around and found herself face-to-face with the harshest-looking woman she'd ever seen. She wasn't tall, but her arm muscles bulged out of her uniform and her face had a peculiar manly quality to it. The nurse motioned for Diana to follow toward another closed door where she stood in front of the keypad and swiped her card. A loud buzz signaled them to enter. Before she walked through, Diana looked over her shoulder and gave Roger a weak smile. He smiled and gave her a thumbs-up.

The squeaky sound of the nurse's rubber-soled feet crossing the highly polished floor was the only sound Diana heard as she followed her down a long, tiled hallway. *This reminds me of jail. I guess it kind of is.* Diana shivered.

Her escort stopped abruptly and pointed to the left. "This is the room where you and Ms. Baker will meet."

Diana wasn't sure what to do next. The nurse flashed her keycard, swiped it, punched in a code, and opened the door. "Go on in. I'll get Ms. Baker." Diana shrugged and thought, *That answered my question.*

Inside, Diana looked around. Opposite a small table with two chairs, she noticed a large plate glass mirror. *Probably a two-way mirror.* Its presence gave her a small measure of comfort. She sat at the wooden table with steel chairs positioned on opposite sides. A short wooden barrier with no glass in between divided the table in half. It was clear no touching was allowed. *Fine by me.*

Harsh overhead fluorescent lights and one frosted window lit the room; but the heavy cloud cover prevented much sunlight from coming through. She shivered not so much from the cold atmosphere, but from the unusual situation she found herself in.

Ten long minutes later, the door opened and Roberta entered the room. Her drastic change in appearance caught Diana off guard. Rather than having waist-length black hair she had often wore in braids, Roberta's shoulder-length curls were unadorned and streaked with gray. She had lost weight and wore no jewelry or makeup. Roberta smiled in greeting. "Hello, Diana."

"Hello," was all Diana could manage to say.

Roberta took a seat and placed her slim hands on the tabletop. Diana waited. "Strange place to be reunited, isn't it?" Roberta said.

Not sure of how to respond, Diana's voice sounded shaky when she said, "How have you been?"

Roberta concentrated on her clasped hands. Her mouth twisted into a crooked smile. "It was hell for the first six months." She looked up. "But after I realized sitting in my room all day wasn't going to change anything, I visited the library. You can take just about any class online, so I decided to study Art History."

Diana's eyes widened in surprised.

"I can see you're shocked. You're thinking, Roberta is actually reading, maybe even getting some smarts. Yeah, who knew?"

"I'm glad you have books and can take classes." Diana shuddered. Everything she wanted to say seemed lame and she felt tongue-tied.

"They helped pass the time. At first, all I thought about was getting from one day to another. But when I realized I wasn't as dumb as I thought, I began to enjoy reading." She looked reflective. "Remember how I used to tease you about studying and taking school so seriously?" Diana nodded. "I was wrong," Roberta said.

"I graduated last month with a teaching degree," Diana said.

Roberta seemed to light up. "That's wonderful. What will you teach?"

"Special Education."

"For retarded ..." Roberta didn't finish.

"For students with special challenges: Autism, Downs, physical disabilities, that kind of thing."

Roberta appeared rattled by her blunder and changed the subject. "I quit smoking,"

Diana's eyes widened. "Great. I'll bet it was hard to stop."

Roberta shook her head. "One of the hardest things I've had to do. But ... think how much money I'll save. Not to mention how much healthier I'll be."

They chatted for a few minutes about nothing earthshattering. Finally, Roberta touched on the core of their visit. "So, have you decided to forgive me?"

Diana had been rehearsing this moment for several weeks. "I have." She hesitated, afraid of how it would come out. "But, that doesn't mean I'm forgetting what you did to me and my family." Her hands trembled in her lap and she stifled a hiccup.

Roberta slowly shook her head. "I wouldn't expect you to, but I hope we can start fresh." Diana remained silent. "After two-plus years of counseling and personal reflection ..." Diana blinked rapidly. Roberta smiled. "I know, shocking. Anyway, I've worked through my past and I think my problems stemmed from my childhood, my mother specifically. A mother's influence, good or bad, is strong and lasts a lifetime." She looked toward the window and closed her eyes.

"It is." Diana sniffled. "We had some good times, though."

Roberta directed her attention back to Diana. "I'm glad you think so. We did. You were my world and I know I didn't do a good job of showing it. I'm sorry for everything."

Diana struggled to keep her voice even-toned. "Maybe Zoë can keep me posted from time to time with how you're doing."

Roberta cocked her head as if she'd hoped for a different answer. "Okay."

Diana squirmed in her seat and cleared her throat. She thought the watchers on the other side of the mirror took that as a sign the meeting was over, because a couple of minutes later a nurse entered. "Time's up."

Roberta sighed and pushed herself up. She brushed her eyes with the back of her hand. "Thanks for coming, Diana. It meant a lot."

"No problem. Take care." Diana watched the nurse usher Roberta out, unsure whether she should follow. Then she heard a voice over the intercom.

"You may leave now, Miss Williams. Your escort is waiting in the hall."

Diana nodded to the unembodied voice. As she walked toward the vestibule where Roger waited, she started shaking.

CHAPTER 37
Wedding Day Reflections

ON THE DAY OF HER WEDDING, Diana woke to a warm, sunny morning, which promised to be the perfect day. She stretched luxuriously in the twin bed in her parents' home and thought about how things had unfolded over the past weeks. A soft tap on her door interrupted Diana's thoughts. "Yes?"

The door opened a crack and her mother peeked through. "Good, you're awake. May I come in?"

"Yes, Mom." Diana scooted up and propped the pillows behind her neck and back.

"We'll be pressed for time this morning. I've already hit the ground running." Emily sat on the edge of the bed. "Nervous?"

Diana smiled. "Not yet, but I will be when Dad walks me down the aisle."

Emily nodded. "I know the feeling. On my wedding day, I did okay until the music began and everyone stood and turned toward Daddy and me. I came close to crying."

"I've practiced this day a hundred times in my mind." Diana paused. "I hope you aren't worried about Roberta ruining the wedding."

Emily reached for Diana's hand and gave it a squeeze. "I trust your instincts. You made a sweet gesture to forgive and forget. We couldn't be more proud of you." She glanced away for a moment. "I pray all goes well."

Diana managed to smile. "It will. Roberta will behave herself. Zoë and Stan won't let her try anything stupid."

Emily chuckled. "I hear he can be intimidating."

Diana switched the subject. "Are the girls awake?"

"I haven't checked on Kerri and Kate yet, but Bryan is rattling around. I think he's in the garage doing Lord knows what."

"I wish Grandma Louise could be at the wedding."

Emily looked wistful. "We gave it serious thought, sweetie, but it would be stressful for her. She wouldn't understand what was going on and I'm afraid the crowd would upset her."

"You're right, I suppose. But Grandpa is coming, isn't he?"

"Yes, along with the rest of the family. We will have a wonderful time," Emily affirmed.

Diana hopped out of bed, yanked open the curtains, and raised the window. "No matter what happens, today will be the happiest day of my life." She smiled at her mother. "The second happiest day."

Emily dabbed her eyes with the sleeve of her nightgown. "I know what you mean, honey."

* * *

Roberta sat in her hospital room and thought about her turbulent history with Diana. She smiled remembering Diana's visit in June. It had helped make up for their showdown in the hospital room following her deliberate overdose five years prior. Rather than being grateful for Diana and Zoë's quick actions that saved her life,

Roberta had lashed out. She had hurled lame excuses at Diana for her *own* inexcusable behavior and tried to gain sympathy. Diana had walked out of the hospital room and told Roberta she never wanted to see her again. Roberta winced at the memory.

The prospect of attending Diana's wedding made her more nervous than when she sat under the gaze of the stoic judge. Her lawyer had prepared her for the worst and held her hand while the judge handed down the sentence of five years in the Oregon State Hospital, followed by five years of mandatory counseling from mental health professionals.

Roberta had cried in relief, and outside the courtroom, she collapsed in Charles' arms. "I thought the judge would throw the book at me."

"You dodged a big one today. Five years. Not a bad deal. Clearly, your psychological evaluations tipped the scale. The judge found the childhood abuse by your father, mother, and grandmother caused irreparable mental trauma and inhibited your ability to discern right from wrong when you kidnapped Diana. Even so, you were as good a mother to her as you knew how. You scored big points there."

"I'm so grateful, Charles. Thank you. Thank you for saving my life."

She had sporadic contact with Charles via emails and phone calls since entering the state hospital, and messaged him as soon as she received Diana's wedding invitation. Her time under medical supervision and counseling hadn't curtailed her audacity and she thought he would jump at the chance to escort her to the wedding. His silence was his answer. She was disappointed, but not surprised.

On the morning of Diana's wedding, Roberta paced her room and tried to concentrate on positive thoughts. She stopped to look out the window, saw a small tree, and smiled at the memory of Zoë's fairy godmother-like blessing following the ceremony of tying a cloth *cloutie* to the dogwood outside her bedroom window.

Could the Cornish tradition have made her three-fold wish list come true? *Probably not.* But she was grateful she had not been sentenced to hard time in the Oregon State Correctional Institution. She was sure incarceration would have killed her spirit and ruined her health; and was grateful Diana had forgiven her for the kidnapping.

Roberta tried to calm her nerves while she waited for Zoë and Stan to arrive. She couldn't wait to begin the forty-eight hour vacation even though it was under Zoë and Stan's strict supervision. They had convinced the director to approve them to accompany Roberta to the wedding and have her stay with them overnight.

The nurse tapped on her door and entered without waiting for a response. It had taken Roberta several months to get used to the no privacy rule. Today she welcomed the interruption.

"Roberta, your friends are here," Nurse Rampling said.

"Thank you." She gathered her small suitcase and garment bag and followed the nurse down the long, tiled hallway. Her heels clicked in contrast to the silent footfalls of Nurse Rampling's soft-soled shoes. Roberta glanced into several open doors and smiled at a couple of acquaintances who gave smiles and thumbs-up in response.

Roberta turned the corner and stepped back to wait for the nurse to punch in the ever-changing security code. Then they headed toward the visitors' lounge which Roberta didn't frequent. She had few visitors, so she spent most of her time with the other patients and online classes working toward her Bachelor's degree in Art History.

Zoë waved to Roberta, rushed forward, but stopped short of her natural impulse to hug her. She stood at arm's length. "I almost forgot, no touching. It's so good to see you." She frowned. "You've lost more weight. Have you been sick?"

"No, I've been hitting the gym three times a week and limiting desserts. Want to look good for my first vacation. Thanks for your help in making this happen."

They met Stan in the vestibule where he took the suitcase and garment bag without a word. *Apparently, he hasn't gotten over my past*; Roberta shrugged at the thought and took Zoë's arm. She felt like a young girl on her first fieldtrip from school.

CHAPTER 38
The First Day
of the Rest of Their Lives

IN THE PRIVACY OF THE MASTER BEDROOM, Emily and Cassie helped Diana prepare for her wedding day. It was the only room with a full-length mirror and the afternoon sun. Both features gave the women the perfect setting to do Diana's makeup and hair, and to help her change from ordinary clothing into her elegant gown and flowing veil.

"I feel like Cinderella," Diana said as she stepped back from the cheval mirror and turned slowly in a circle. The long, slim skirt followed her movements as subtly as a ripple on a lake. "What do you think?" She asked her mother and best friend in the mirror's reflection.

Emily clasped her hands to her breast and sighed. "Perfect."

Cassie nodded. "You look beautiful, Di."

"Today is everything I ever dreamed of." She twirled again, this time with a flourish, and stopped in front of Emily. "All I need is a basket of fairy dust to sprinkle on everyone as I walk down the aisle so they can feel as happy as me." Diana spread her hands downward and brushed her ivory-colored dress as if to scatter motes of fairy dust. "The silk is so soft I can hardly feel it against my skin."

"And it's as light and airy as angels' wings." Emily added, "You made a good choice."

Coming out of her reverie, Diana automatically looked at her bare left wrist and asked, "What time is it?"

Emily glanced at the bedside clock. "It's 2:30. We'll have to leave within the half hour." She focused on Diana and smiled.

"Is Daddy getting the limo?"

Emily nodded. "Don't worry. He and Bryan left in plenty of time. They should be here any minute."

"Can Kate and Kerri come in now?" Diana asked.

"Yes, please. They've been hounding me for hours to see you in your wedding gown. Cassie, will you bring in the girls?"

"Don't forget the handkerchief Mrs. C gave you," Cassie said.

"Oh, it's in my purse. Thanks for reminding me. Even though she couldn't be here, I'd feel terrible if I didn't carry it with my bouquet."

* * *

An hour and a half later, Diana stood at the entrance to the Portland International Rose Test Garden in the West Hills with Glenn, the father of her heart, holding her left arm and James on her right. She held the calla lilies in her right hand and tried not to let it shake in anticipation and nervousness. Diana took a deep breath. *I can do this.*

She missed seeing her mother being escorted down the aisle to her seat in the front row; but watched Cassie and her sisters precede her in their strapless, knee-length black satin dresses. She smiled as Krissy, Roger's niece, scattered yellow and white rose petals along the freshly cut grass. Krissy's little dress was cream-colored, the same shade as Diana's short sleeved, silk gown. The flower girl's blonde curls were held in place with a crown of yellow roses and baby's breath. Diana's fourteen-year-old brother, Bryan, stood up front next to the best man and nervously tugged his collar.

Diana tried and failed to stifle a hiccup. James asked, "Are you doing okay, sweetheart?"

"Yes, Daddy." Diana peeked at him through her veil; then she turned and smiled at Glenn. He gently squeezed her arm in response. She had dreamt of this day ever since she was Krissy's age, but all the dreaming and planning hadn't prepared her for the jumble of emotions. Never once did she think *both* of her fathers would be walking her down the aisle.

The sun had dropped behind the tree-lined ridge and the harsh daylight softened to a pre-dusk glow. Distant birdsong combined with the murmurings of the guests helped Diana remain composed. The calming effect was like theater lights dimming just before the curtain was raised. She smiled inwardly. *This is a play and I'm just one of the cast.*

The Williams family and their guests sat on white wooden chairs on the left and Roger's large family filled up every chair on the opposite side of the aisle. Violin bows were poised; the conductor raised his wand and with an outward motion of his arms, the six-piece orchestra played as one. Everyone stood and turned toward the entrance, which cued the fathers and daughter to take the first step along the long, fragrant pathway.

Roberta, Zoë, and Stan sat near the aisle toward the back. Diana glanced over and her first thought was Roberta looked a decade younger in her sapphire blue long-sleeved dress and stylish hat. Roberta smiled at Diana. Zoë held a white hanky at her throat and gave Diana a wink. Stan's height and bulk looked out of place in the row of women; he nodded and his right dimple hinted at a smile.

Diana's heart beat faster as she approached the gazebo, which sheltered the pastor and her bridegroom who shifted his weight from one foot to the other. His blond hair was slicked back and glistened under the twinkle lights hanging above. Diana smiled remembering how he had worried about Portland's humidity wreaking havoc with his unruly hair. She momentarily took her eyes off Roger to acknowledge Maggie sitting next to her mother. Maggie blew her a kiss and wiped a tear from her cheek. Tears welled in Diana's eyes and she sniffled. She felt James' hand tighten just a tad, as if to say, *You'll be okay, we're almost there.*

Diana watched as her mother smiled and unsuccessfully prevented a hiccup. When the three paused in front of the gazebo, the pastor said, "Who presents this woman and man to be married to each other?"

In unison, James, Emily, and Glenn said, "We do." James gently kissed Diana's cheek, as did Glenn. Then the men took their seats next to their wives.

Roger stepped next to Diana and the pastor continued with the ceremony, which was interrupted twice: first when the best man dropped the ring, and then more dramatically when a low flying robin swept through the gazebo narrowly missing the pastor's head. The audience chuckled in relief and a few minutes later, after the exchange of vows, they burst into applause as the couple kissed. Diana raised her bouquet as if in victory and Roger pumped his left fist. Then they joined hands and smiled all the way down the grassy aisle to meet with the photographer to take wedding photos.

An hour later, the wedding party took several vehicles to the World Forestry Center in Washington Park for the reception and dinner.

After the multi-course meal, which Cassie had helped plan, breaks for the photographer, and the cutting of the cake, Roger and Diana took to the shiny, oak dance floor followed by couples of all ages.

"I feel like putty in your arms," Diana said as she gazed into Roger's eyes.

"And I feel like I could hold you forever," he responded. Diana felt his arm tighten around her waist and she laid her head against his chest.

When the orchestra took a break, a disc jockey stepped in to play contemporary music and happily took requests from the crowd.

Diana and Roger stopped dancing, sat at the head table, and watched the delightful scene. "Mom, Dad, this is so fun. It looks like everyone's having a good time, even fussy Miss Brown." Diana pointed to her parents' long-time neighbor whom they had lovingly dubbed *Mrs. Kravitz* after a 1960s television character.

James leaned around his wife and said, "Your mother was careful in choosing her table mates. I think Miss Brown is flirting with Mr. Tabor."

Emily playfully jabbed her husband. "Miss Brown doesn't know how to flirt."

"You never know. Weddings have an effect on women. She might see this as her last chance to find a husband." James chuckled. "I think Miss Brown has had her eye on him for a long time."

Roger stood, smiled, and held out his hand to Diana. "You've rested long enough. May I have the next dance?"

"If it's a slow one. My feet hurt." She slipped her foot from under her gown and rotated her ankle. "I should have listened to Cassie and bought shoes with lower heels. I had trouble walking on the grass and tippy-toed all the way down the aisle."

"You can switch shoes, dear." Her mother brought out a pair of satin slippers from a large purse she had tucked under her chair.

Diana smiled. "Thanks, Mom." She was poised to get up, but stopped when she saw Roberta walking across the room toward the head table. Silence fell over the group when Roberta stopped directly in front of Emily and James. Diana felt the air turn electric.

"Mr. Williams, Mrs. Williams, I'm Roberta Baker."

The visibly stunned couple silently nodded and waited for her to continue.

"This may not be the right time, but I won't have another chance." Roberta paused. "Thank you for inviting me." She smiled at Diana. "You look so beautiful. The ceremony was perfect, even the birds couldn't stay away." She looked at Roger. "I hope you and your beautiful bride have a wonderful life together. Diana deserves the best."

"Thank you," Diana whispered when Roger didn't respond.

Roberta leaned across the edge of the table to speak with Emily and James. "I did a horrendous thing when I stole you daughter, and can never make up for your pain and loss. I am truly sorry and hope one day you will forgive me," she said, *sotto voce*.

Emily appeared speechless; however, James spoke up, "We appreciate your confession and apology. It has taken a while for us to work through our loss, but our family is doing well now."

Roberta stood tall and brushed the skirt of her dress as if to remove the last of her guilt. "I'm glad. Thank you again for your generous gesture in inviting me and for letting me speak." She slowly turned and walked back to the table she shared with Zoë and Stan.

Roger broke the silence. "That took a lot of nerve for her to come up to the front table."

Diana thought about the double meaning of Roger's comment before she asked her parents, "Are you okay?"

Emily cleared her throat as tears spilled onto her cheeks. "I've dreaded and dreamed of this moment for years, but who would have thought it would happen on Diana's wedding day?" She dabbed her eyes with the linen napkin.

James leaned in, gave his wife a hug, and said, "It seems strangely appropriate, though. Weddings are a sign of a new beginning, and Roberta helped us to forgive her and move on. I feel like a huge load has been lifted from my shoulders."

Emily lowered her head for a moment, and then fumbled through her purse for a tissue.

"Mom, you've been so brave." Diana scooted her chair over and put her arm around her mother's shoulder.

Emily wiped her eyes again. "Thanks, sweetheart." She sighed. "That felt awkward, but I guess you're right, James. It couldn't have happened in a better place, or at a better time. We certainly don't want to make a scene." She smiled and appeared to stifle a hiccup.

Diana laughed. "Mom, I feel hiccups coming on, too."

"It's time to lighten the mood. Let's dance." James held out his hand. Emily stood, took his arm, and they entered the crowded dance floor.

"Are you ready for more dancing, Mrs. Archibald?" Roger asked as he took her hand and gently pulled Diana to her feet.

"Wait a sec. I have to change my shoes." After a moment, she said, "Ready!" Diana slipped into his embrace and they joined the crowd who were dancing to May I Have This Dance for the Rest of My Life?

THE END AND THE BEGINNING...

ACKNOWLEDGMENTS

It doesn't take a village to write a book; however, for me, the process includes family and the myriad skills of fellow writers and first readers. First of all, I want to thank my family for being supportive and helpful at every stage of my writing career.

Thank you to Barbara Seiders, Editor-in-Chief of Seiders House Publishing; our Tuesday night critique group; and my team of Beta readers: Paul Eslinger, Diana Langner, Judy Arndt, Kandi Wyatt, and Becca Knudsen. Without their expertise, Heartbeat Interrupted would not be the book it is today.

ABOUT THE AUTHOR

Donelle Knudsen carved out time to write while working full-time as an executive assistant to a financial advisor. She often rose during the wee hours of the morning to complete her first book, *Rose City and Beyond*, which she gifted to family and close friends. Over the years she has written poetry, award winning short stories, one non-fiction book: *Through the Tunnel of Love, A Mother's and Daughter's Journey with Anorexia*, and two novels: *Between Heartbeats* and *Heartbeat Interrupted*, the second book in the Heartbeat series. Donelle loves to travel and spend time with family.

To contact Donelle Knudsen:
- Visit her website: http://donellemknudsen.weebly.com
- Facebook: https://facebook.com/DonelleMKnudsen/
- Twitter: @donelleknudsen
- LinkedIn: Donelle Knudsen
- Goodreads: Donelle Knudsen